All The Things That Could Be

A Novel

Cullen Cantwell

All The Things That Could Be

© 2024, by Cullen Cantwell. All rights reserved.

No part of this book may be reproduced, distributed, or transmitted in any form or by any means, including photocopying, recording, or other electronic or mechanical methods, without the prior written permission of the publisher, except in the case of brief quotations embodied in critical reviews and certain other noncommercial uses permitted by copyright law. For permission requests, write to the publisher, addressed "Attention: Permissions Coordinator," at the address below.

cullencantwell@gmail.com

ISBN: 979-8-218-46551-3

Cover Illustration by Stephanie McBryde (thanks mom.)

Cover Text by Emily Wolk

For Clementine and Ari:

You are the lights of the world.

Mommy and Daddy love you

"One person can make a difference, and everyone should try."

— John F. Kennedy

All The Things That Could Be

1

James Dalley finally got a lunch break; there were moments he didn't believe it would ever come. As he enjoyed his few moments of freedom, he continued to reflect on a quote he had fixated on earlier in his shift: "More connected than we have ever been." That is what they say. Truly, modern marvels of technology are the devices that allow us the opportunity to ensure that our circle doesn't depreciate as rapidly. We can force those relationships to exist as if they were on ventilators. Perhaps, one day, we can remove the tubes that keep them breathing and those relationships will exist on their own again, but perhaps not. Sometimes these devices highlight loneliness, sometimes they make it worse.

James believed this deep in his soul. As someone who emerged from his adolescence with an average number of friends, he had felt the attrition of time dwindle those relationships until one day he talked with someone not knowing it would be the last time. This understanding that relationships end over time was not something that he didn't comprehend, but one that stung him a little bit more each time it happened. Relationship creation meant eventual relationship death – always a tough pill to swallow.

Reflecting on these truths, James sat quietly in his car, the low hum of the radio broke the silence to remind him he wasn't totally alone. As he took small bites of a

All The Things That Could Be

flattened sandwich, he thought about the most philosophical things he could think of – questions with no answers. Questions that he had no answers for, at least. He pulled down the mirror from his visor and checked his face. He had mellow, hazel eyes complimented by a short beard. His hair always laid in the perfect way – perfect being the way he wanted it at that moment. He had a narrow face that looked like God started with a home plate and made adequate adjustments.

Rain began to patter on the windshield, a harmonious and rhythmic sound, something that always put him in a better mood. It was a reminder that sometimes the sun goes away, but it will come back out. It is a time for reflection and reprieve, a time to grieve. A nice little timeout for life. James felt like these rainy days were increasing, like a perfect transition into spring. The sun was coming out less and less, and the rain wasn't bringing any flowers.

The clock rolled over another minute and indicated that the brief freedom from labor was about to expire. Noisily he rolled up his bag and stuffed it in his pocket to throw it away. More delicately, he placed his phone and keys into another pocket, braced himself for the rain, and opened his door. The water made a dash to get inside the car as if it were seeking refuge from itself. James swung his legs outside, planted his feet onto the cement, and pushed himself out. Locking the door behind him, he strolled back toward his work, ready to conquer the second half of the day.

All The Things That Could Be

It had been a good while that James Dalley worked as an associate at his little slice of labor. The pay wasn't putting him in an impressive tax bracket, but at the end of the day, he was able to go home and not think about work until the next time he showed up at it. He was now a manager, however. He had taken time to try other careers, the first one was being a teacher. However, the work was long, the pay wasn't great, and the take-home stress felt like a second job.

There was always something that some kid was dealing with that was hard not to take on. The most important part of the job was the relationships you would create, so it was tough not to be empathetic. However, sometimes the weight of the sadness would permeate outside of work hours. They never prepared you for that in school. He was able to shoulder the burden for a few years and seemed to be successful in his career, but the emotions were too much, and James was ultimately too sensitive. Maybe it was because he was young and idealistic, thinking that helping take on that burden would be the panacea the kid needed. But, one day they are in your class, and the next day you never hear from them again. You only have to hope that everything turned out okay and that you don't see their name in the papers.

The beauty of this job – the pay was similar, and James didn't need to play the savior role. The relationships he had with customers were almost always joyful – nothing like the underlying darkness that existed and was spilled to him by early teenagers – problems he had no answers to. Sometimes it felt like he had given up on an entire generation of people who needed him, but the flip side was to be cannibalized by his own thoughts. Ultimately, it was about tearing off the band-aid and looking out for himself.

The bell dinged as he entered back into the store and saw the familiar faces – some customers, some coworkers. As soon as he entered, one of the associates set a path directly to him. The young worker was a teenager with dirty blonde hair who took long strides to get to his boss. His movements were purposeful, and his demeanor was serious – work was serious.

"Blake, what's happenin'?" James anticipated the young man and wondered what the cause of the haste was.

"Shipment arrived in back. There is nowhere for it."

"Shipment? We don't have one coming today."

"They are here now, said they contacted you."

"Well, they didn't. Alright, hold on." Annoyed, James turned around and started to head toward the back of the store. He quickly swung back to the young blonde.

"Wait, go get Jamaal and have him help you move Sunday's freight over to the overload spot. We will have to do this quickly. I'll be back there in a bit." He quickly turned back around the other way. "Lizzy! Can you handle it up here? I need to go to the back to help move some stuff around."

The older associate, Lizzy, had been working at the store since its inception when James was in high school. She never desired a higher-up position like management, this money was play money for her and her family. She may have worn the same thing for the last ten years – a tattered, red, long-sleeved shirt with blue jeans and a pair of Nikes. No doubt the shirt was the same, but the jeans and the shoes well could have been the same model, but there was no way to tell without asking. She stood balanced upright against the register as a few customers strolled about the store. Slowly her head turned, and she looked toward James, who had already made his way to the back. "Sure thing, honey." James didn't hear her, but he knew what the answer was going to be. He knew the inflection she would use. He knew that he could depend on her.

In the back, Jamaal and Blake were already moving the freight. James stopped and looked at his hands. He looked up at the young men who he had seen multiple times a week in the same capacity for the last few years or so. He thought about the same, boring lunch he had packed. He thought about the rent coming up. He thought about his youth and the dreams he once had.

Today was simply the continuation of the previous day, the day before that, and the day before that. There seemed to be no reprieve from his monotony, every day was labor for a little bit of money to pay for the little bit of freedom he had. He knew that he wasn't the only one who lived like this – which made the reality easier and harder. Easier in the sense that he wasn't alone; harder in that made him quite alone.

He thought about the life he lived and the emptiness of its future. James had nothing on the horizon. "What kind of life is this?" That's a question that he often ruminated on.

Be that as it was, James stepped toward the men who were visibly shaking – a fact that embarrassed him, he should have been there sooner to help them before the work got tough.

"Christ, man, what is in here?" Jamaal said with his face stretched as much as James had ever seen.

"I don't want to know," James murmured. It was true – James had no desire to ever know what was in the boxes. He knew that he would, however – a fact that depressed him. In his mind, he decided that at some point he would no longer know what was in the boxes. He would no longer know the dimensions of the store. He would no longer be able to remember Lizzy's perpetual garb.

One day, he would leave. A silent, grand spectacle. He would disappear one day, and no one would know but him.

2

All too many times in his career James would take on the soul-crushing news of others. Some of these people he knew, and many of them he didn't. Like so many other people in his life, country, and world, he was exposed to a catastrophic amount of information daily, so much of it falling under the category of "bad news". He would take that news, and then do what with it? It was another question that he often struggled with.

As a teacher, he had often been confided in by kids who were struggling with issues such as bullying at school. The best he could do would be to encourage them to report the incident. He knew kids who didn't want to get caught often had a tough time being caught, so the advice wasn't very helpful. No one could help unless they could them red-handed. He felt that the solace that he could deliver as a trusted adult was so little, he felt like he had failed them.

Just because you receive that information on the clock, doesn't mean that when you check out, it stays at work. He found the lives of the students and the issues that they had so heavy it felt oppressive. What can you do about a kid who you know is homeless and has a vague understanding of where his next meal might be coming from? His answer was "not much". He could act as a stopgap for only so long before realizing "I am not going to be able to pay my rent.".

All The Things That Could Be

Driving down the road, going into a store, or sitting down at home, you are inundated with more and more news. Things that you can hardly escape and things that you can do absolutely nothing about. An entire country is starving to death because of religious strife and war. A house fire engulfed an entire family. Rent has increased and it has caused families to start moving into shelters, or under bridges. "What am I supposed to do with this information?" A fair question.

With all the bad news came some good news, and even the good news was bad news. A woman manages to beg the Internet enough to pay for another month's rent after her husband passes away due to lack of access to a too-expensive medicine. People cheered their contributions and felt as if they had saved a person from a harsh reality. "What am I supposed to do with this information?"

Sitting at a restaurant waiting for his food, James watched the evening local news and counted seven stories, book-ended by commercials, every single one of them was a story of loss, death, sadness, grief, or tragedy. An entire culture and its news cycle was dominated by bad stories of things they could do little to nothing about.

The stickiest of traps, you were given the information that you didn't want, and you had to think about it later because it was so horrific. If James, an adult, was having a tough time handling this, what about the most impressionable minds? Growing up and seeing that everything around them is awful and sad, and then expecting them not to be? How does one even suggest they do that? Keep them away from the news? Keep them off their phones?

There was so much of this in the culture that it started to bleed into the kids' normalcy, James believed. The most awful stories were made laughable by students, they would pass it off as something to razz one another about or to make a snide comparison comment in class. They were being raised on bad news, except to them it was just news. Maybe, they didn't understand it as being "bad" because it had always been normal to them. Or, perhaps, the world had always been bad, and this was the first generation who was not duped into thinking it was a benevolent place or had even been such a utopia. With this, students created realities in themselves that would be predetermined as bad, everyone was miserable, and so by default, you had to be as well.

Find bad, magnify bad, live the reality.

One did not need to only watch the news to see the hurt that existed in their society, they only needed to drive downtown and there would be no denying that what was being shown was very real. There seemed to be no solutions, either. "What am I supposed to do with this information?" Nothing. The changes that you made in life were so localized, and the pain of the world was so much, that, like spitting into the ocean, the effect was irrelevant.

These thoughts would sometimes consume James and leave him spiraling for a few days at a time. He struggled with handling the pressures of the world and occasionally would find difficulty in accepting being content in life knowing that pain and suffering were just around the corner. He tried to rally each day, as a teacher, but ultimately, this mental stress became too heavy for him.

After only a few years in the classroom, he decided to dial down the stress and left the education position he had held. Instead, he decided he would work at a local store, quickly bumping up into a managerial role – the job wasn't very difficult, at least in the emotional baggage aspect. The pay cut, seemingly, outweighed the lack of stress in the job.

However, there was also a feeling that he was passing the buck, or quitting on people, which was tough to stomach sometimes. Some of the success came from developing an "out of sight, out of mind" mentality. It all seemed wrong, and it seemed tough, but he would tell himself, "Sometimes we do what we need to survive."

James bid his time while he figured out a plan to escape, whatever that looked like. He also recognized the likely reality that this, too, may have been a passing phase and that he wouldn't feel like abandoning anything and everything he knew was the solution. Feelings are fleeting and acting purely on them was a fool's errand. He knew he would need to see how he felt in a few weeks to make a more honest assessment of his state. He had felt uneasy for years,

All The Things That Could Be

so while feelings were fleeting, a feeling crept into the recesses of his mind, slowly growing like a shadow on a sunny day – he never saw it get bigger, but then he'd turn around and realize it had.

Walking into work, he noticed Jamaal lounging in the breakroom, a vacant expression set on his face, James' entrance into the room went largely unnoticed. James kept his eye on the seemingly hypnotized man while he stuffed his coat into the locker, rain droplets still clung to the jacket. Making more noise, purposefully, than usual in hopes of breaking the spell cast over him. The tree stayed rooted to the breakroom couch, roots that were keeping him from moving, and they were deeply entrenched into the fabric.

"Hey," James softly crept into his view, as not to startle him "You good, Jamaal?" Suddenly, as if he were transported thousands of years and thousands of universes in an instant, Jamaal face contorted in the form of shock and surprise. In a way that mimicked bringing his head out of ice-cold water, he snapped back to reality, "Ah, man, uh yeah. No, I'm good. Just chillin'." The answer was satisfying but the voice wasn't.

"Yeah, I am not too sure I believe you there." James ribbed back to him.

"I said, I'm fine." This time the voice matched the answer, he meant it. He delivered it sharply and like a high-pitched whistle, it told James to stay away. Wanting to respect the invisible fence that had been set up but also knowing that something was up put James into purgatory he had lived many lives in – wanting to help, but not being able to do anything and thus resigning himself to nothingness.

"I hear ya. Loud and clear. See you on the floor, Jamaal." He had found in his young life that using someone's name could have a great impact on the relationship. In this instance, however, Jamaal returned to his self-induced comatose state and James made a mental note to keep an eye on this throughout the day. His workmates were some of the few relationships he maintained, so he tried to put work into them while he was still present.

Back out on the floor, James emerged and made his managerial rounds, a routine he adopted soon after his promotion, it was a combination of making sure things were tip-top in the store, checking in on his employees, and seeing how they were doing. He had received a supermajority of "good", "fine", or some rendition of those words which acted less as a true reflection of their lives but as a polite courtesy that was said to move the conversation along. This was a delicate dance because there were days when he felt he should inquire deeper with "No, how *are* you?" but the thought of the consequences that may follow kept the question at bay.

Walking through the aisles and making notes on a clipboard he brought around with him; he noticed the size of the notebook. He flipped back to the beginning of the notebook and saw it was the same information page after page after page. The same markings just different products. He was living a life of absolute repetition, a droll existence of stocking shelves and replacing products for a meager salary, and the people he managed made less.

"What kind of life is this?" Again, the question reverberated in his skull like an alarm. He couldn't stop thinking about the phrase in the context of his own life. Did people enjoy this kind of monotony? What was the purpose of this all? When was the last time he had a truly joyful experience that he could reflect on, one that was not marred by the stains of awful news somewhere? Perhaps, this was growing up and he was faced with the reality of life. This is just what you did. This is what people do as human beings. Most people.

Certainly, there was a very minute portion of the population who had evolved past everyone else. They worried neither about time nor money. Would the top of the power structure eventually become the dominant species? Just as homo sapiens eventually overtook the rest of her ancestors, would the mundane, overworked, underpaid, suffering, and struggling people eventually be taken over by those who weren't and didn't?

While he continued to make his rounds while ruminating on these issues which had existed since time began, surely, he wouldn't be the one to solve them, his ear turned to a situation that was developing near the front of the store. It began as a low and unintelligible muffle from where James was standing, but soon the noise and clarity permeated the shelves and became very clear to the manager. He heard Jamaal's voice and another voice, unfamiliar to him, bouncing back and forth like ping-pong. James tucked his clipboard under his arm and made his way to the front at a semi-hurried pace. As he moved closer, the situation seemingly was escalating, almost devolving into yelling.

A couple of other employees had made their way out, drawn to the commotion like moths drawn to a flame, hanging around noiselessly. James attempted to ascertain information in real-time to figure out the problem.

Jamaal turned to him with his arms out and a face mixed with panic and anger. "Man, Jimmy, this guy here is saying that bought this jacket here and is trying to return it – I ain't never seen it before. We don't have it! He won't get out of my face about it." He turned back to the customer and continued, "Man, I am telling you, we don't have it!"

The face of the customer was as red as a cherry, and he was sweating, looking like he was ready to pop. James knew at that moment that this conversation was going to go poorly for the balloon as Jamaal had one of those minds where if he said it, then it was. He could spend fifteen minutes looking at an inventory list and he would have it memorized. The fact that he had worked at the store for more than a year meant that he might have been aware of not only what inventory was in the store but also the quantity.

All The Things That Could Be

"My son said he bought this for me from here! This…boy…is calling my son a liar!" The man had calculated a sentence when broken down was seen as using innocuous words, but when pieced together carefully worked on two different fronts: it was used to demean his intelligence and subtle racism, the kind you could argue had plausible deniability if you were arguing with someone who didn't push back too hard. In his mind, he begged for Jamaal to not take the bait.

On its face, what was being argued was not worth getting to that level, and if they all settled down, they would see it to be true. But when you're in the conversationalist's fight or flight mode – few choose the latter. James saw Jamaal begin to wind up in his chest, he was going to give the main exactly what the man wanted. As his mouth began to open, James stepped directly between the two, "If he says it's not ours, it's not ours. Get out of my store and don't come back. Got a problem with that…email someone." His suggestion was the best he could do in the moment of sticking up for Jamaal but also feeling frustrated. Although a much thinner build than his current adversary, James was inches away from the man's face. Jamaal began to unwind.

The message sent by James was received, and the conversation began to deescalate. The man tried to get in some last jabs, but James knew how the situation was going to play out. By then, another coworker had come and secured Jamaal from any further actions. The man left with his shirt and Jamaal left with his dignity and sanity.

All The Things That Could Be

These interactions were the worst. This wasn't the first time James had ever had to deal with some squabble or misunderstanding that had threatened to erupt and scorch the countryside, leaving scars on it for the rest of forever. In the moment, it seems like winning the argument, and being right, is the most important thing in the world, it's the only reason to exist in that moment. But when you stepped away and realized it was such a useless waste of anyone's time and to have put effort into keeping that fuse lit was shameful. The age of being right.

Unconcerned with anyone who witnessed what happened, James set off to find Jamaal. He was in their original meeting place that morning, but he wasn't as rooted anymore. Shook up from the encounter, still excreting rage from his body, Jamaal paced back and forth in the room. It wasn't any surprise that James handled it the way he did, his employees had always been fans because they knew he supported him, even in the face of the almighty dollar.

"Man, I'm sorry, I shouldn't have let that guy push my buttons like that." Jamaal started, still pacing, but slowing down to have the conversation with James.

"Nothing to apologize about, that guy was in the wrong. I am sorry you had to deal with it." James spoke calmly, hoping the effects would wash over him and provide further salve. A lengthy silence hung around in the room with the two of them, its presence as obvious as a third person.

All The Things That Could Be

James decided to excuse the unwelcome third party from the room. "So, what happened out there? That isn't you. You were acting a little weird this morning when I saw you, and if you don't wanna talk about it, I respect it. But I am aware, and I am concerned." He sounded like a parent.

Jamaal let out a big sigh and buried his head into his hands and then groaned, one that crescendo-ed into something that resembled a growl. He then ripped his face from his hands. "Ah, Jimmy. I went to the doctor's the other day, they found something and decided to biopsy it and send it to a lab. I haven't heard anything yet. But if it is cancerous, I don't know how I'm gonna pay for it. Either the cancer is going to kill me, or the debt is." James was teleported right back into the classroom. This burden he would carry with him after he left his shift.

"I…don't know what to say. I am really sorry that you're dealing with this. I don't know what I can do to help, but if there is something, please let me know." He stood next to him near the break room couch. "If you want to hang out or need time off, whatever it is, keep me posted."

"Appreciate it, Jimmy." He sank into the couch and James took that as a sign that he wished to be left alone at that moment.

There was no shortage of questions that James could have asked. There was no question that he could ask that would alleviate the worry and pain that was pumping through his veins. The cortisol had turned up to eleven. He let it be.

"Don't tell anyone, man. I don't need everyone knowing about this." Jamaal pleaded weakly.

"I got ya. Keep me updated." James nodded to him.

***

Carrying the burden is never easy. Some people possess the ability, the skill, to shed the problems of others, many times by necessity. People already have so much to deal with, what is it to take on the issues of others? You have your stuff that you presumably haven't solved, what is the good in taking on someone else's unsolvable enigmas? James always silently championed his empathy, but there was no shortage of times when he wished it didn't exist.

The region showed its true colors that evening as James made his way home from work. The clouds were thick and gray, they threatened a storm, which wasn't uncommon, but following through was rare. The rain and the darkness created negative feelings in many people in the area, it was a darkness and drollness so predictable at that time of year that it became culturally ingrained in the region. Seasonal depression would hit a lot of homes, and the pulse of the town seemed to slow down. Where people had walked, they now moped; where people had chatted, they now griped, where people had lived, they now existed.

Pulling into the supermarket as his last stop before home, he did not attempt to shield himself from the rain, it was like trying to defy death: entirely futile. While he let it be known that he respected the inevitable, he attempted to subtly cheat it by walking a bit quicker, even skipping up onto the curb.

Passing the pumpkins in a large crate outside, he moved passed a woman, curled up near the carts. She was covered in clothes that had not been washed or dried properly for a while. There were gashes in the clothing, which didn't help considering she was ill-equipped to handle the weather as it was. A Pandora's box of goods lay next to the woman, neither she nor her miscellaneous goods impeded anyone's freedom of movement, but he knew that people took alternate routes when they saw her. He felt guilty because his first thought was to avoid the human who had fallen on hard times, but he had to make a conscious decision not to.

She lifted her head from the dry, plaid blanket which, on many occasions, she hoped would turn into a magic carpet and whisk her away if she thought about it hard enough. "Can you spare a dollar?" she asked James with a voice filled with no expectations.

"Sorry, I don't carry cash." It was a true statement, he typically didn't, but he said it with such low effort as if saying "I don't have cash and I have no intention of pulling out any cash. Heck, I don't even know how I would get cash!"

Just one human to another, asking for a little help, a little decency. The other human in the situation is just glad to not be in that situation. The prone lady's predicament, how did she get there, and how close was James, or anyone else, to being in her spot? How many missed paychecks was he away from having to ask strangers for money? One, two, three? The number was not many, and there was a realization that the difference between that human and himself was potentially not as big as he felt safe with.

The doors sensed his presence and welcomed him into the shelter he may have been seeking, they didn't know, they just did their job. Grocery store noises filled the grocery store air. Customers toted their metal carts up and down aisles, occasionally making small and insincere conversations with other patrons. Sometimes avoiding the conversation altogether by acting like they were trying hard to locate that very specific product on the shelves that eluded them.

Meandering through the sections of the store, he picked up the usual list. He ate the same meals quite often. His lunch was always the same. His health was no worse and no better, so he purchased the same hygiene and other assorted goods. He knew exactly where each of what he was going to buy was located. At the checkout, a once familiar voice greeted him.

All The Things That Could Be

"Oh hey, Mr. Dalley!" He took one look at the kid and tried to put a name to a face, by adding a few years to every student he ever had. Like a slot machine lining up a winning pull, he was able to come up with the name for the face.

"Oh, hello there, Asher, I didn't know you worked here. How are you doing?" The teacher-student relationship was no longer a requirement since he was no longer a teacher and the student had either just graduated or still with another year to go, he couldn't remember. However, students often felt that at the very least, the formality of the relationship must be observed, if for nothing more than upholding tradition.

"I'm good! Yeah, I just got this job. I figured I could pull a little extra money before college next year. I know I will need to save a lot if I hope to go."

James thought, "If you hope to go?" and then responded, "Well, you were always a great student, and it would be a shame to see you not pursue academics at the next level." Asher's abilities in the classroom on his worst day were often better than most kids on their best. "Thanks, Mr. Dalley." A sheepish smile swept across the cashier's face. "Anything else I can get for you?"

"Yeah, give me a twenty-five-dollar gift card there, please."

All The Things That Could Be

The two, now social equals, said their goodbyes and said their well-wishings. James made way with his all too familiar grocery conquest to the parking lot, but held the gift card out in his hand, ready to give it to the woman who probably had wished she never needed to rely on such charity. When he left the store, he noticed the rain had ceased, but the chill in the air hung around – a dark fortress encircled the sky, and the spot where the woman once found shelter had left. The blanket and box of random goods stayed there, but the woman was absent. Where she was, he could not guess, so he laid the gift card on the blanket. She would find it when she returned.

Pulling out of the parking lot, he drove down a back road. Puddles inhabited the roadway, and a film of water seemed to be on everything his headlights touched. Driving further into the darkness, his lights spotted someone trying to stay on the shoulder, but it was too narrow, and they had to veer into the road. As he got closer, he realized the clothing, inadequate for the weather, and knew it was the lady asking for a dollar. She marched toward the darkness. They were at least a mile away from the store at that point, her leaving the warmth and her belongings couldn't have been by accident.

"Where is she going?" The answer may only have ever been known to her.

3

"We have to start cutting back some hours." A line that James didn't want to hear, especially because it was going to fall on him to deliver the unfortunate message to those it impacted. To argue about the statement was to act in futility, he knew this, but to not say anything would have been an abdication of his responsibilities as a boss. "What do you mean, Pam? We have hit all our numbers the last couple of months, with comfortable margins, too." Pam sighed as if the question inconvenienced her. As owner of the store, she believed that she ultimately held all the cards and negotiating power.

"Well, rent is going up, and things are getting more expensive, this is just a decision that I have to make." It was a half-baked answer without any sincerity behind it.

"Would you like to be the one to tell them then?" James quipped back. Pam's eyebrows arched, feigning that the insolence displayed amused her. She placed her hands behind her head and rested her head in them before delivering the final blow. "No, as manager, that is your job. Please make sure it happens when I give you the list. Do you have any suggestions?" What a cruel ask. James shook his head.

The question seemed to be a test because, in her head, she had already made the decisions. Three employees were going to drop below full-time hours, which would end up having a bigger effect than just the hour reduction. Jamaal's name was highlighted in James' mind when he saw it, he blurted out, "You can't drop Jamaal below full-time. It can't be him." He stopped short of telling Pam why, as he remembered what he promised Jamaal, but wondered how much flex room existed, given the circumstances.

"Oh? Why is that? Do you have another suggestion?" Another cruel ask, sacrifice one lamb for another. James' mind went into overdrive as he tried to consider his options.

"Give me one month. Let me try and push sales and bump numbers. If numbers aren't up, even more, then I will personally make suggestions that will capitalize on making sure you keep your best workers intact." Acting as if he were withholding some information that had a direct impact on profits was a bold strategy, but if it worked, he would be able to buy Jamaal and a few others some valuable time. Pam was indeed intrigued by the power play, and as she once believed that she held all the cards, she now found out that there were some scattered amongst her workers. She acquiesced to his request.

Committed as he was to the health of the store, any time Pam came in with her nonsense, James felt a little more divorced from the situation. He knew that for most people, the job was certainly a stepping stone and not a career. However, as a stepping stone for some it was vital, and missing it from their lives could have extreme consequences and cause a complete halt in their career or life progress. To James, it seemed that Pam had forgotten how important the hours and benefits were to many of her employees. If it were costing her bottom line, she seemed to forget even harder.

The meeting ended and James felt like he needed to shower. He felt dirty for having to concede a plan to eventually hurt one of his employees. He sent out a text message to the workers to confirm their monthly morning meeting the next day. He emphasized that it was important they showed up since there was news that concerned everyone. That night, he practiced in front of the mirror what he would say to them. He had three different takes and knew that he would choose the right one when the time came.

***

Early the next morning, James rolled through the morning fog into the parking lot. Sunrays poked through the low clouds, illuminating some parts of the store and failing to touch others. He went through the opening routine and set up the chairs in a cleared-out portion of the store. A table skipped clumsily along the cement floor as he compiled a soft breakfast of muffins, donuts, coffee, and juice for his people. They slowly filtered into the store. Those whose shift would follow the meeting prepared the store for opening, and those whose shift didn't, offered help to James or sat around talking about a hodgepodge of topics.

Once seven o'clock rolled around, the team found their way to the circle. As was tradition in these meetings, while James was getting the introductions and agenda down, everyone served themselves. They would sit in the uncomfortable, metal chairs, accepting the discomfort in exchange for brevity and food.

A few minutes into the meeting, he decided to make headway on the topic that would be most pressing for some. "Pam and I talked yesterday. She is looking to reduce hours – taking three of us down in hours, is what I could glean from it." This was a lie, as he knew exactly what and who was going to be selected. "It was supposed to go into effect immediately, but I asked for a month to see if we could push our sales and bring in more money, hopefully offset the cost and make this a non-issue." James managed to look each employee in the eye at some point while saying it. A message that could have been construed as "You're the chosen one. Listen to me because if we don't do better, you are toast."

"Bring in more money? I thought we were doing pretty well." Lizzy correctly pointed out. She knew they were doing well, she handled money all day. Her uncertainty was done as a courtesy. Others mumbled back and forth.

"You're right. We are. We have exceeded all our numbers." James bluntly stated, frustrated by the thought. "You have all done excellent, and cutting any number of you is going to bring sales numbers down. It's a short-sighted solution, but she is dug in." He slapped his knees with his hands, and a loud clap reverberated throughout the store.

"I would update your resumes and just put feelers out there. Some of you may feel the sting this go around, but some of you may be victim of this in the future. I just don't want any of you to be blindsided when it happens." There was a tinge of vindictiveness in his voice, and they could all sense it. Thinly veiled behind his words was the message, "Get out of here. This place isn't worth it", and while he may not have intended to say as much, the unintended message was interpreted loud and clear.

The meeting adjourned and James caught up with Jamaal as he was heading back towards his car. "What's good, Jimmy?" A classic Jamaal greeting.

"Hey, I don't want to alarm you too much, but…" James looked from side to side to ensure that the conversation was staying private from eyes and ears, he covered his mouth with his hand, "I saw that list, and you were on it. It would have bumped you from full-time to part-time, I tried to buy you a month. Even if we kill it with these numbers, I bet people are still getting the boot." A look of dismay washed Jamaal's carefree smile away. He looked at James with a look that was gauging his level of seriousness.

"I am not kidding. I know you're worried about what little coverage you have, well, I thought this would probably make it worse. I am sorry, Jamaal." James removed his hand from his mouth. He reinstructed him to do what he told the rest of the crew, and if he needed a reference, to put him down. The face on Jamaal was, again, vacant, much like he saw the other day in the breakroom. "Alright. Thanks, Jimmy. I appreciate it. I just need a moment to myself."

James nodded and stood still, letting the upset man decide what his next move, and consequently James' next move, would be. With a thousand-yard stare, and a million questions coursing through the deepest regions of his brain, he turned and opened his car door and sat. He didn't move for as long as James was there.

4

Always on time, always ready, always doing the right thing. These were tenets Jamaal Jackson tried to live by. Perfectionist as they were, and some naysayers would argue, elitist to some degree, he was usually able to function accordingly. From primary school to college, he worked tirelessly to ensure that his best was given, knowing it wouldn't always be noticed or appreciated. Whether it was academics, sport, or some other medium of exertion, he was known as someone you could count on.

Graduating summa cum laude a couple of springs prior, he had achieved a task never attained by any members of his family tree: getting a college education. Raised by his father, he was always supportive of his ambitions but also made sure Jamaal was walking a path of success, in his eyes that meant being college-educated. But what came after college was difficult. A local job market that all but rejected him in the field he was educated in. The opposite of lucky, he came out of the job market at a time when layoffs were happening, and unemployment was climbing – especially in the biotech industry. He had chosen a difficult path, in part because he wanted to make his dad proud, and the information came easy to him.

However, colleges didn't help him much in the way of securing salaries. After he got the ceremony and he did the dance, he was put out into the arena of man and expected to go at it for himself, like so many. Most of the jobs he applied for, he didn't even qualify for as far as requirements went. A lot of those jobs, he didn't even bother applying for, until someone said these companies hire outside of those guidelines all the time. He felt silly that perhaps he had missed an opportunity.

He would keep his applications relatively local, trying to find something, anything. But the bites never came. He would get an occasional phone interview, but it never passed that. Whenever he asked for feedback, his lack of experience was offered as a reason. In his head, he questioned, "Where am I supposed to get this experience if no one wants to help me get experience?" He went so far as to ask this question to someone letting him know that he was not going to be moving on to the next round of interviews, to which he was told, "Volunteer work is often a great spot to start."

"Volunteer work? When am I supposed to volunteer when I got to pay bills?" Volunteering indicated that he either had excess money or time – he didn't. Quite frankly, he didn't know anyone in his immediate circle that did. The concept of giving up your time to give someone free work just so you can put it on a piece of paper was silly to him.

Working in town, he helped run a local store that sold anything from anti-freeze to fire pellets to flannels to board games. The pay wasn't bringing home a huge amount of money, but it was working as a bridge while trying to get a job in his expert field. He paid rent to his father, but he typically stuffed it into a jar for him to have later. He talked about going back to school, he thought he could wrangle enough scholarship money to make it happen pretty pain-free. But being fresh out and having his hopes dashed time and time again would take its toll. He was learning how to handle the rejection in real-time.

He had never had to deal with the idea much, considering he was always someone that people clamored for. Everyone wanted to be his partner in class, everyone wanted him to be on their team in sports, even colleges upped one another to try and get him at their school. When he graduated, however, he was thrown into the job pool and sunk immediately to the bottom. He had no idea how to swim, that took experience. So, he sat at the bottom of the pool, air bubbles periodically escaping, hoping that one day he would learn how to swim.

Working at the store sucked up his time, and the small town possessed few biotech firms in or around it, his life was at a standstill. He was still getting older, but he didn't feel like he was getting better. Two lines on a graph, progress and age – both should always be moving in the same direction, he reasoned. He began to stress about the situation to the point that he felt ill. And then he continued to feel ill. And it never really went away.

Bringing this up at home was how he knew it could be serious. It was very rare that he ever expressed serious concern about something he was dealing with, he had always figured out whatever was going on, so the fact that he couldn't with this, brought him consternation. His father's face moved back and forth from concern to worry to suspicion. Ultimately, he suggested he take it to the doctor, the one answer that Jamaal begged he wouldn't hear. He heard him and he listened.

On a cloudy and chilly day, he made for the clinic and met with a doctor. Jamaal explained what he was feeling and when he began feeling it, trying to convince the doctor that this was indeed stress, and they could shake hands and be on their way. After some questions and some probing, the physician became concerned about something he felt in his neck. The concern was great enough that he ordered an immediate sample to be taken so they could biopsy it.

"I am feeling this bump right here." He poked at it and Jamaal felt it with his own hands. "Typically, these kinds of bumps are benign, but we need to take a look. Is there any history of cancer in your family?" The questions he was asking felt void of humanism. They were just questions that he could ask and not worry about having to answer himself. Jamaal felt upset by it, but it may have been paired with the fact that his answer was not going to help calm his mind.

"Yes, there is." He said quietly.

"Ahh. Yes. Okay, well we will see, and we will let you know." The doctor continued to probe his neck while asking nonchalant questions. A brief procedure occurred and then he was on to the next patient to ask medically necessary questions in a disconnected tone.

He gathered himself and left the doctor's quarters, his head hanging low as he processed the information just given to him and thought about all the possibilities that lay before him, and the possibility that he wouldn't need to worry about it at all. He was frightened by it all.

Back in his car, he took out his phone and made a decision that he knew he shouldn't. He opened a web browser and began looking through the possibilities of what he was facing. He knew better than to do this, but he couldn't help himself. He needed to start putting a timeline on his own life if that was going to be in his near future. He suffocated himself with information, most of it probably not even applicable to himself.

With the asphyxiation of the job pool and the self-strangulation he was currently involved in, he knew he had to take himself to work.

He skulked into the store and sat on the breakroom couch, unable to move or fixate his attention on anything other than a mark on the wall. A complete statue on the outside with a million thoughts processing in his brain in a moment. Worry and dread ripped through his mind, and he could feel it in his stomach, he knew that he would never be hungry again.

All The Things That Could Be

That night, he talked with his dad about the visit but also an unhinged customer at the store that day. The whole event tipped him over the edge, an incredibly uncharacteristic reaction from Jamaal. He felt as if he wore the weight of the world on his chest. He had no appetite, and even though his father implored him to eat, there was nothing he could choke down at that moment that wouldn't immediately show back up.

More bad news poured in when found out he was going to be on the chopping block for hours at work. The little health insurance he had was about to be wiped out. His boss told him he had about a month to figure things out – a gesture he appreciated, but now he was in a state of panic and anxiety. He sat in his car after the conversation and stared at the horizon for an hour or two. There was nothing to do in that moment except exist.

After his moment of existence, he felt he needed to rally and formulate. He had lost his touch of being resourceful and initiative – a couple of traits that always made him the star pupil, athlete, and on and on. Driving home, he talked himself into a better state of mind, an old habit that helped pull him out of tricky situations before. Positive mental attitude. Once he strode through his door, he went to the bathroom and splashed water on his face, looked at the mirror, and said, "Let's go, big boy."

Maybe it was the urgency of death by cancer or by debt that awoke his inner drive which had been dormant for so long. Maybe it was the natural cycle that he was no longer in tune with just awakening in him to do well. Whatever the cause, a couple of old-fashioned techniques he used as a kid and young adult rebooted him like a powerplant long dormant, once the lights were flipped on, production was imminent.

Job searching had always taken place in a specific locality – one close to home. He had never explored something too far away from his hometown and in an instant, the world opened like an oyster, and it was his job to find the pearl.

He spent the days he wasn't working, and the nights that he was, scouring the Internet for openings. To broaden his horizon, conservatively at first, he worked in concentric rings. A fifty-mile radius, a two-hundred-mile radius, a one-thousand-mile radius, the entire Milky Way. The further away from his hometown that he went, the more nerves would strike him. He applied to anything and everything that may have been relevant to biotech as the scope of his position broadened. He had always intended on pharmaceuticals and medicine, but now he was checking out a wide breadth of potential work.

One position specifically caught his eye, even though it was highlighted and warned against the solitude and loneliness of the position. In Greenland, a newer biotech firm was studying bioremediation in response to a recent oil spill in the North Atlantic. The application warned against the darkness, daylight would be minimal, if at all.

"Interesting." He said aloud. The thought of living somewhere it could be noon and pitch black out at the same time was intriguing to him. The pay wasn't listed as fantastic, but the lodging and food would be taken care of. There was even a hospital within fifty miles that could furnish him with the necessary procedures, should he need them, probably. The position had been posted for a couple of months, which told him that the warnings of perma-darkness may have been off-putting to many of the potential applicants. He applied and emailed the director of the project.

***

Seven days later after his initial doctor's visit, he was still waiting for the results. He tried to convince himself of the positives of the situation – the doctor got good news and was just too busy to call, but the urgency was dulled because it was benign. With all good, there is the reverse, and he thought that what they found was so strange and foreign that there would be no cure, and it was being sent off to be examined, no time to call the who had harbored it. Neither scenario realistically existed, but his mind would keep busy with it when he wasn't daydreaming about curing cancer in Munich.

All The Things That Could Be

He stepped up his pep at work, the simple, good things he had discovered were outshining the fact that he could be dying. Ultimately, there was nothing he could do about it, he would just roll with the punches. If he understood James correctly, he was on borrowed time at work. While he was roaming the aisles, looking for someone to assist, his phone started to vibrate. He never brought his phone with him to the floor, but he had been expecting the call at any moment. Fate delivered. His hands trembled and all of the sudden his feelings of carefree-roll-with-the-punches-nothing-I-can-do-about-it-anyway were non-existent. He was now at the mercy of science and biology.

He stepped off the floor briefly and locked eyes with James and Blake, one who was aware and another who wasn't. One who showed no surprise that the man who never carried his phone on the floor, was, and another who couldn't put the pieces together. Jamaal pointed to the phone as he answered it and James nodded and walked away, toting Blake along with him.

"Good morning, is this Jamaal?" He could tell it was the same doctor that saw him. His voice was sharp and gave no clues as to what the diagnosis was.

"Good morning, yes, it is." His voice was something above a whisper as he choked on the message through the phone. "I assume you are calling with news for me?" He got straight to the point, making sure the man didn't deviate from the goal.

All The Things That Could Be

"Ah yes. We received the diagnosis from the lab today."

This discussion was brief. When the phone call ended, his shoulders dropped and he exhaled, then slumped into a chair. James came around the corner.

"I need a moment."

5

He was born loved. He was raised loved. Throughout his life, there was never a question to James as to whether his parents loved him or not. They made decisions based on his interests rather than his wants. They gave and withheld accordingly. He was praised and disciplined according to fair norms and mores. He also felt robbed.

James moved slowly through the front door of his apartment, one he shared with someone he met via a posting in the local newspaper. The living situation was amicable – especially since he worked during the day, and she worked a graveyard shift. She worked in aerospace, but he had no idea doing what. Since she was splitting rent with him in a small, dingy apartment, he guessed she wasn't in charge of engineering, but he never thought further about it than that. Her name was Emily, and she was a quiet and kind woman. Three years his senior, she came from Georgia, and they felt like their first meeting was good enough to trust living together for a year. That year was almost up, and they had not explicitly discussed renewing their lease, but with the small conversations they had had about it, James felt like it wasn't going to happen. He was alright with this – especially more as of late.

As he trundled towards his bedroom, he dropped his backpack onto the floor. The bag made a loud thud as his backup boots smacked the ground. Since it was a bottom-floor apartment, he lived a life of luxury in this way. He always tried counting the advantageous moments of his life, but they were few. He walked into his room and sat on his bed, instantly burying his head in his hands and deeply exhaling. He was exhausted by the perpetual merry-go-round of life: the sights all the same and he could never get off the ride. Now and again, he would shift to a new horse, but the journey was always the same, the destination was never reached. He was born tired.

On his desk lay a journal and next to that journal was a photo of his parents propped up in a frame. Both of his parents were killed instantly by a drunk driver two years prior. People said that the pain would dull over time, but over time never happened, as the pain was fresh each day. The loss of his parents made James re-evaluate a lot in his life, including leaving the teaching profession. He decided he would rather live a simpler life – doing too much was just too taxing at this point in his life.

Waves of sadness crashed upon him whenever his sea was calm enough to allow it. Times of solitude seemed to invite the storm. Keeping busy was a blessing and a curse. A simpler life brought simpler times, but also stormier seas. James recognized that not everything made sense when it came to handling his grief. The conversations he had about it were minimal. He had no other family in the area, only an extended family in a far-off land. Could have been Seattle or

All The Things That Could Be

Portland, could have been Jupiter, it didn't matter because they didn't talk anyway.

His journal opened to a page of scribbled-out words. Scribbling in graphite indicated half-cooked ideas, while lists in ink indicated serious plans. At that moment in time, everything was graphite and messy.

Leaving would be a wonderful idea – although it wasn't an idea he had fully planned out. He felt like there was a bit of genius in that, let the journey take him where it did. There was excitement in this process, and he felt like he would find a product along the way. To the East Coast – New York City or perhaps Maine…those were details for the future.

His parents would have no doubt been perplexed by the plan, as would have been an earlier version of himself. But things changed and they changed quickly. A time of loss – not just of his parents but of himself as well. He stayed close to his parents through high school, college, and when he was a young professional. He felt unique in this regard, but he realized that his relationship with them wasn't like that of his peers. However, he also felt normalized by it. It always brought him great serenity. Now, he felt great sadness and instability.

***

All The Things That Could Be

For the last six months, James had saved every spare penny he had made. Now, he had begun selling off possessions to make money. He knew that holding on to some of these things would be useless. The fewer possessions the better. He just needed cash to ensure the journey continued as long as it could. He would enjoy it until he ran out of cash. He hoped to find purpose on the way, a new place to settle or a new job. However, he was ready to let the chips fall where they may.

The more and more he thought about it, he continued to land on the same thought: irresponsible and stupid. Still, a sense of freedom came with it. In his mind, admittedly, the plan was short-sighted, and he was most certainly better off staying put. Yet, he felt that things managed to have a way of working out the way they were supposed to. He wasn't going to stay happy here, and he felt a calling to leave this place. Go somewhere, anywhere.

He began to empty his closet, selecting what items would make the journey and which ones would not. Every piece of clothing sorted into its new destination brought him closer to a decision to leave. With this came excitement, and with that excitement he knew that folly would be present if he wasn't too careful. Still, he could feel the carelessness in his acts.

After he sorted out clothing and other goods into the bring and donate pile, he sat down at his desk. James blindly fumbled through the drawer and found what he was looking for a pen. He put the ballpoint to the paper and let the pen bleed for a little bit. He had once toyed with the idea that once it was in pen, there was no going back. With the best penmanship he had ever produced, he sent the pen across the top line: three months.

Excited and feeling resolved, he stood up, stretched, and then relocated to his bed. He knew he would miss the bed. Visualizing himself getting into his car and pulling out of his town, it wasn't long before he drifted off to sleep. When he awoke, he penned out a list – compiling more of the scribbled graphite notes into something that made sense.

6

"There are a lot of maps here. Which ones are best for travel?" James looked at the rack of maps knowing that if he looked long enough, he would find the answer to the question, but also knew that asking would save him a significant amount of time. He was in a saving mood.

"Local? Regional? National? Global?"

"Um, national."

"Third from the top, second from the right." The clerk didn't even have to look up, which impressed James. Either people still buy a lot of maps, or this guy was well-versed in his craft, a trait that James appreciated.

His dad had always been excellent in his craft, and he was a champion of quality labor. His father was a long-time union man working for the railroad, and although things weren't always excellent for them as organized labor, his father would never talk negatively about it.

James had decided he would take a phone with him, but he refused to use it for anything except emergencies. While he wanted to leave the old world behind, there were some concessions he was ready and willing to make. It was the biggest point of contention for himself, but he knew that he could bring it and not be tempted by it – there was nothing on the device that was so sacred to him that he would be persuaded to use it. The pictures of his parents and his youth were backed up on a hard drive.

He selected a book that had a large-ish map of every one of the fifty states. He knew that most of the book would go untouched, "who knows, maybe one adventure leads to another." Let the chips fall where they may – maybe something changed, and he would roller skate through all fifty states raising awareness for a good cause.

His mind snapped back to where he was. He looked at the clerk, in a jerky motion clutched the map to his chest and said, "Thank you, sir!" in a most upbeat manner. He ran his card and was on his way.

When James got home, he entered his apartment in a very foreign way – bursting through the door, the inside knob crushing the pad whose sole purpose was to protect the wall. He strode to his bedroom and quickly but neatly cleared off his desk before sprawling the map book across it. He felt like a mix of Bilbo Baggins and an old history teacher he once had who was always excited about maps. But unlike these people, he was rather inexperienced in looking at them, but he would figure it out quickly. He just needed to know roads and towns – if those things were there, he would be set.

The amount of money he had accumulated over the last few months would suffice for a decent-sized adventure. He hadn't mapped out exactly how long because he didn't know exactly what he would be doing. He knew that he

All The Things That Could Be

would be sleeping in his car to save money and buying adequate food to eat along the way. James figured that his biggest money spender would be on gas. He would be frugal, but he also recognized that he was out to enjoy an adventure – money would be spent on things he didn't anticipate. Part of the fun was the in the unknown.

He felt that he owed it to his co-workers to give them ample notice, so he started to write out a departure schedule. Four weeks would be plenty of time, and it matched up with his lease which expired in two months. The time would allow him to keep saving money and prepare mentally and physically for the trip. As he began to finalize his plans, considerations continued to pop into his mind, and he penned them down as they came. The plan was coming to fruition. A great adventure awaited.

As he continued to compose his list and clean up his possessions, the front door to the apartment opened, and in walked his roommate. He walked out to the living room and greeted her with an unusual energy – this was odd, and she knew something was up.

"Hey, I know that we hadn't really cemented plans for extending the lease, but I got the feeling that we were not looking to do another year?" he trailed off and leaned slightly, unsure of how the comment would land. The roommate, Emily, had an unchanged face and body language which suggested she was unphased by the comment.

"Yeah, I suppose not. I was going to ask if you wanted to, I know we still have a couple of months." Her answer didn't match her perceived body language. James shifted uncomfortably, not wanting to inevitably disappoint.

"Ah. Well. The thing is, I am leaving." James' words danced clumsily out of his mouth.

Emily's demeanor changed from stoic and unphased to slumping and disappointed. Her long, brown hair fell softly over her face as she lowered her head and stared at the ground.

"Well. Alright. Shoot." A staccato of words came from Emily. She then lifted her head back up and staring at James quizzically she said, "Leaving? Where?"

"Well, I am not sure exactly. East Coast? New York? Maine?" He didn't sound confident or convincing in the least bit.

Picking up on this uncertainty, Emily began to wonder if he was telling the truth or had already selected another living partner and didn't want to hurt her feelings.

"That's pretty vague, James. What is going on? Are you messing with me?" She didn't think he was playing a joke, but the conversation was unsettling to her.

"Yeah. I don't know exactly. I just feel like I need to go out and be free. I feel constrained by the day-to-day routines that I am stuck in. I think I need to go out and just experience something that isn't necessarily...scripted?" He searched for the right word and felt "scripted" was as accurate as he could be in that moment without taking too much of her time.

"I am not going to lie to you James, it doesn't sound like the best plan you have ever had. I mean, at some point, we get older, and we settle into the monotony of the day-to-day. That is just kind of what life is." Not that she had known too many of his plans in life, as their relationship was limited – this conversation was one of the deeper ones they had ever had.

"You're okay, right? This isn't like, you, wanting to...not live...anymore, is it?" The sincerity came through in her voice, even if the sentence wasn't the smoothest that had ever been muttered. She looked around sheepishly – almost embarrassed at the amount of concern she showed.

"What? Oh my...no. Of course not." James retorted – the thought had never crossed his mind. Death was the last thing that he wanted – vitality and happiness were his focal points.

"Oh. That's good. It's just...odd. You don't have a destination, which makes me think you don't have any working prospects or housing prospects. How much money do you have...or, at least, do you have enough? What happens when you run out?" Emily was talking to James as if he were an older sister who was genuinely concerned about his well-being, this sense of care toward his well-being was received warmly and he suddenly wished he knew Emily much more than he already did. He smiled at her.

"It's going to be an odd journey. I don't know what I expect to find, or if I expect to find anything at all. Maybe I will fall backward into a new career or a love of something or someone, and maybe I will run out of money in the middle of Iowa and must figure it out. Either way, it will be like nothing I have ever done." James spoke about the trip with more confidence than he had ever thought about it. As soon as he finished saying it, he tried to decide whether he was convincing Emily, himself, or both.

Her beautiful face started to turn the longer they spoke about the plans, and her attitude towards the plan became less critical and more curious. James didn't detect it, but she began to romanticize the idea herself. She realized it was outside of her comfort zone and it scared her to death to think of herself not having stability, even if the price was monotony. However, she then imagined herself selling her car as a last-ditch effort for cash and wondered how little the underside of an overpass resembled a Best Western, and how long she could stand extreme hunger before she cried.

It wasn't that James hadn't thought about these things, but more so he believed he could overcome them. He figured he had conquered worse and that his instincts would take over and prevent him from having to experience such extreme maladies. He felt a lot of trust in his instincts, which hadn't placed him into the most ideal current scenario. But this felt different, he had never been tasked with survival, and when it came to that, he believed in him.

Between the two of them, James felt like he had turned into an anarchist. Here she was, bound to the rules and laws of society, strangled by its mores and norms. James was free and she was not, he had the upper hand to speak about anything he felt – she could not. He could bend the rules of time and the tales of history without consequence, she was still confined to all of these "truths". The feeling made him whimsical.

"Well, if you wanna come with. Lemme know."

"Ah. I don't think so."

"Well, cool if not, cool if so."

Nonchalant. No rules. Middle class, safe anarchy.

7

A lot of people who win the lotto don't come out and say it. However, there are always signs. Sometimes it is just the freedom from crushing and unrelenting debt and a temporary break from wage slavery, and if you play your cards right, you emancipate yourself from it entirely. The emancipated walk differently, you can't always tell exactly what changes, but you notice it.

He was slowly casting off the chains of wage slavery, but he did not possess the parachute that most people who were emancipated did. That was the difference between him and them. He didn't require a fallback; the freedom was enough – as short as it may be. It may be a short time before the social contract of man shackled him up again, but they were denied at that moment.

With one week until his departure date, he had accumulated significantly more amount of money than he originally planned on going out with. Solidifying plans ahead of time certainly had its benefits. The amount of information he decided to give to people seemed to be following celestial calendars. Or perhaps it just had to do with the person, he hadn't thought too much about it.

In James' world, there just didn't exist enough people to tell who would hold on to that information for any useful amount of time. A couple of his co-workers would care, so he would give them the lowdown – their feelings about the

All The Things That Could Be

success of the adventure varied from face to face. Their respectful skepticism was in bloom because they liked James, so the words of warning that he received were like spring showers in the Pacific Northwest, they were anticipated and braced for – but the actual rain wasn't anything that anyone couldn't handle.

The most information he gave was to Lizzy, her opinion was as predictable as her outfit. As he drove into work, he would have bet every dollar he had made on what she was going to wear and what she was going to say.

"Sweetie, you sure 'bout this? That seems a little…concerning." Her slow words crawled between the two and he was able to fully comprehend her words by examining her posture: one arm balancing her on the counter, one leg ceremoniously behind the other – seemingly casual, but it was the position that allowed her to do her best thinking. "You okay? You need anything? You need to talk to someone?" The pace of her voice quickened; it could have been said that the words now strolled over to James. Concerning.

The question was put with kindness and concern, but James figured out quickly that this was going to be a theme of his trip. He understood the concern and understood why people may have thought that way, but as far as happiness went, and as far as clarity was concerned – he was on top of the world.

He left a message for Pam.

All The Things That Could Be

I am leaving. Makes the decision easier for you. — James

***

Emily ultimately denied James her company, something that didn't bother him so much as it wouldn't have elated him if she chose to go. He saw benefits and downfalls to each, so he decided that neither option would perturb him. Although she had started making suggestions for him on his journey: places to visit, places to stop to sleep, where he could shower. She felt like she was constructing a map for a treasure hunt where she had no idea of the destination or goal. Perhaps she would suggest too many stops and would leave him bankrupt on the side of the road 10, 100, or 1,000 miles out of town. James took it all as suggestions. With a week to go, he at least had opened his book of maps.

He studied the map intently, as if there were states he had never seen before, and roads were a new concept he had never considered. He traced the lines with his fingers as if they would physically bring him to a place he had never been. For a moment he felt like an old explorer, charting a journey across an unknown land. Land never touched by anyone, no Indigenous people, no accidental explorer, no colonizer – nothing. The kind of explorers that exist only in television and stories.

All The Things That Could Be

Every day that passed was another one closer to the beginning of the journey. The excitement was building as he pored over his maps and marked every single YMCA he could find along I-90 (the preferred route thus far). These were good places to take a hot shower and get some exercise to help prevent any muscle atrophy that may have lurked in the shadows. The YMCAs were the first places that James considered when he began thinking about this journey. If you could live from Y to Y, you would do just fine. He may not be able to hit one every day, but that was fine.

One day, he woke up and it was time to leave. His keys dropped silently into Emily's calm hands. They hugged briefly as she wished him good luck. Perhaps this was the last time they would ever see each other. The neophyte cartographer brought his marked-up treasure map and himself to the car and drove away, uncertain if he would ever return to the Pacific Northwest.

8

There is something about being born in the rain and of the rain. The rain brings about solitude. Rainy day? Best stay inside. It acts as a natural barrier that prevents us from connecting. In this way, it explains why people in the Pacific Northwest are often described as cold and uninviting. They are not, they are just used to being kept at home because of the rainy days. Why get all excited about doing something when you know that the rain could put up a wall between you and said person or activity at any moment? Life is what happens between the rain delays.

Having become an expert at solitude and quiet – as many Pacific Northwesterners are – James reveled at the thought of the long road trip, sometimes not passing cars for miles, which gave him a feeling of comfort and belonging. Sometimes he even deviated from the main road to take some backroads that would lead him back to the main road forty-five minutes later. Whether he was doing it for the enjoyment of the ride or to borrow some time and figure out his plan (the product had not yet presented itself, the process was in control), he could not say.

The rain beat down on the car as if it were a parade snare drum. The windshield wipers did what they could do to repel the potential invaders and assist in giving the driver a clear view. James did not worry about the raindrops; a name that seemed too gentle for what he was experiencing. The sound brought him peace and happiness. He welcomed them as friends. He never used an umbrella.

As he zigged and zagged across the state, he hoped that the rest of the trip would be like this. He could drive into a storm and never come out of it, and that would be fine. Just continue driving through downpours until the end of time. Whether that was right-brain or left-brain thinking, he didn't know. He wasn't even convinced that that was a thing – much like the adage that you only use ten percent of your brain. He had heard it before but was carefully skeptical in his head. Never would he say it aloud, never know who was listening nearby.

The first night on his trip was not the first time he slept in his car – it was something he practiced for two weeks leading up to the departure date. He had looked up ways to ensure he stayed warm, without making his car look like a teenage den of sin. Despite the research he did, there were some learning curves: the perfect amount of blankets, where to position them, how to sprawl out, how to not fog up and wake up feeling like you're in the Amazon Rainforest, what to listen to, when to keep the car running, where to park, where not to park, what to keep next to you, what not to keep next to you, how close it should or shouldn't be. There was a lot to consider.

Anyone who has ever had to sleep in their car and did it without preparation learned quickly that it's not a game that you can just play without practice. Those who think they are masters of the art are humbled in heat or in frost.

Since he didn't pack too much, space wasn't too much of an issue. He was able to fold down his backseat and throw down a makeshift mattress. He planned to park near people who he knew were doing the same thing: a strength-in-numbers kind of mindset. Truck stops seemed ideal – they would understand his situation. Stay away from anything open twenty-four hours, lest you want to be visited by three ghosts every night…sometimes more.

He tested for two weeks in a relatively controlled environment, one without much weather or temperature variation. He figured that he could adjust for variability by adding and subtracting blankets and be just fine.

The first night of the journey he stayed at a stop in the pass where the weather quickly turned to temperatures that he had not practiced in. That first night hinted that the journey may be liable to produce unforeseeable circumstances that he would need to adjust to quickly, as well as foreseeable circumstances to someone who knew what they were doing. James was not of that crowd, however. What is a journey without a little learning, thought?

He parked in a rest area which was mildly populated, by his guess, as far as rest areas went. He parked close to some of the idling autos, but not too close. He didn't want to seem desperate and didn't want to encroach. Unfamiliar with the norms of the trucker community he wasn't sure if everyone had a de facto assigned seat, and he didn't want to be the new guy coming in and accidentally marking yourself for death by inadvertently starting the revolution (even though most people dreamed of doing it, you were just the one to do it, albeit accidentally).

He made up his bed in the back of the car, carefully rearranging the puzzle of his possessions. In the car, in the most confined space he could take up residence, he knew that cleanliness and orderliness would be paramount to his success. A dirty and messy setup would have him back home scouring the streets and aerospace factories for Emily, begging her to wave her wand and create another room in her, presumably, new apartment to let him back. His success would partially lie in executing tasks he had always been great at. He grabbed his book, he had brought four, and settled in for the night. He flicked on a USB light and began to soak in the words of another journey from another adventurer far away.

He noticed outside that snow started to dance around his car. A dance that would be performed all night. "How absolutely wonderful." He had always loved the snow, it reminded him of the holiday season – when everyone was one percent nicer to each other.

He tried to battle to keep his eyes open. Serendipitously, his vision was perfectly aligned with a lamppost which allowed him cozy, front-row tickets to the roadshow. But the ballet of white slowly changed into a mosh pit. The hum of diesel engines from a few other patrons to the show soon was enough to whisk James away into a slumber.

Time moves quickly when one sleeps, but you can't prove it. You just know that it does. Even if you were to fall asleep and the person next to you stayed up all night, your experience of time is different from theirs. And if you believe Rene Descartes, then you believe it to be even more true.

In his blinking of time, snow had piled up at an alarming rate. The temperature dropped rapidly, and the easily foreseen circumstances were in a mood to teach a lesson to anyone who didn't respect weather enough to consider it every day.

9

James woke up in a freezer. His entire body ached from the cold and his face felt like it might as well have been outside. His windows were covered in snow, and he no longer could see the lamppost which displayed the most serene sight mere hours before. Yet, he didn't care to see that sight either. He had trusted the serenity to stay as such, and it turned on him. He fell asleep and, like an assassin, it moved quietly and discretely to snuff him out. It almost got him too. He was lured into a sense of peace and woke to a dangerous and bleak world. "There is a lesson here." He had to believe that.

He continued to hear the idle diesel engines and now he was as close to absolute zero as he had ever been, he understood why they were still running. He felt duped and embarrassed. Yet, he knew there was a lesson here. Some things were going to happen that he should have known but didn't. He would need to adapt accordingly and move on. To survive this journey (what survived meant in this context he didn't know, at this point, it was run out of money alive), James would be required to be smarter than the self who set off on it. He would need to consider options he never had before, he could not be lulled into an early grave (whatever grave meant at this point) but would improvise and overcome as necessary. Failure (whatever failure meant at this point) was not an option. He had burned the ships and would not return to a life of boredom and monotony, despite

All The Things That Could Be

the setbacks he may face (maybe, just maybe, I should have stayed in my bed at home rather than be freezing to death in a tin can in the pass, he considered).

He fought the constraints of the metal cell to put on another sweatshirt and pull his jacket over it. He had packed some thermal long underwear and managed to thrash his legs through them before putting on another pair of sweats. Most important was a couple of pairs of socks. Once he looked like he was ready for an arctic excursion, he toyed with the idea of just going back to bed, or at the very least picking up his book.

After catching a glance of himself in the rearview mirror, he decided to crawl up front. Fumbling around for his keys, he eventually found them and turned his car on, blasting the heat. He had overcome. He wanted to open his door to see how much snow was truly out there, but his doors were frozen shut. Not good. But not the end of the world, "I can just drive down to town if I need it." He assured himself. This felt like the giving up lite version. Town was an extension of the safety of home, he could not do this.

"No going back. Once I pass a town, I won't go back to it." He was making up rules for his own game. Saying them aloud, James felt, made him more likely to abide by them. He wondered how many rules he would make on the fly to help ensure his success. Any version of rule-breaking would be met with consequences from the Games Committee – which consisted of himself and how he felt at that moment. The consequence would be to head back home, licking his wounds, and hoping Pam still hadn't hired someone that she was willing to accept his pity begging to get his job back.

As the car began to thaw out, he got a look at what Mother Nature had given him last night. Outside must have been at least a foot or a foot and a half of snow. The parking lot seemed to not allow any newcomers since he had been asleep, but also no one else had left.

"Uh-oh." He wondered if the mountain pass had been closed since he was up here, and what that might mean for the adventure. He turned on the radio and searched for a station – preferably boring AM talk radio; it was his best hope. Being up in the pass was like two worlds of radio colliding, but then an ebb and flow of what stations came through were garbled messes. A lot of waves were reaching him, but they all sounded like the same unintelligible static.

Ah! He remembered! There was a station that surely would be broadcasting where he was – he just had to remember the frequency. He knew *about* where it was, so he scanned the dial at the low end of the AM spectrum until he came across it. You drive past those signs almost every day and never think twice about them. Things like "When light is flashing, tune in to 770 AM" get seared into your brain without you knowing it.

James had always found the station a bit eerie, the light even more so. The light could be a mundane notification that a fender bender had occurred, or a stalled

All The Things That Could Be

car was holding up traffic and to prepare accordingly. But what if it were more serious? He wondered if it might be the way he learned of a nuclear strike (already happened or incoming). One thought leading to another, he wondered what kind of day nuclear Armageddon might fall on. Anytime he read about it or learned about the Cold War in school, it was always portrayed as happening on a nice, bright, and sunny day – one where kids were playing in the cul-de-sac when the second sun robbed them of their innocence. But what if it happened on a rainy day?

The monotone voice relayed the message with no hope but with no panic either.

"Tahoma Pass is closed. Severe snowstorms through Tuesday. Updates will be made accordingly. Anyone stuck on Tahoma Pass should take shelter. Stay warm. Do not leave your shelter…Tahoma Pass is closed. Severe snowstorms through…"

James spun the small-knobbed dial to anything far away from the station and let out a sigh.

"Well. Shoot."

The sudden storm had entombed James and if this was one of those "special experiences" that you could pay for but have the safety of knowing you were going to be okay and things wouldn't spiral out of control, he would have thought it great. He was a little more concerned right now about the problems he could foresee, never mind the ones he hadn't even thought of yet.

He started by doing a quick inventory of his current food supplies, which were adequate. He had just started his journey and had not dipped too much into his supplies yet. He immediately had acquired a freezer – not that he had much that needed to stay frozen, but now he felt he had options with some of his food and drink.

Before too long he realized that going to the bathroom would present itself as the first obstacle. He, foolishly, never anticipated being trapped in a blizzard so early and had no way to take care of business when it came calling.

Ring, ring.

The sun started to come up, well, maybe. It started to get lighter out there and James could only assume that the sun was causing that. Tough to tell for absolute. It felt like no heat existed outside (or inside when he was frozen awake) so he felt fair in believing that the sun *may* not exist at that moment. Time would tell.

He put some muscle into trying to open the door and managed to get it after some pushing. But the trap was sprung as plenty of snow made a break for the warmest place it could find, his lap and driver's side door. "Damn it." He brushed off the snow as quickly as he could while new snow blew into the car. He quickly picked up on the realization that he was fighting a losing battle and pushed the car door open all the way, not an easy task with how much had been accumulated. He shut the door and ran to the bathroom. He had gambled on turning his car off or not but figured that everyone who was there was nestled in their own private and portable bungalows. The wind ripped through the pass and the snow fell gracefully and then it looked like the start of a 100-meter track race, but with thousands of lanes and racers.

James had lived relatively near a mountain pass his entire life, but he did not know or even suspect the weather to be so foreign. He felt a strange sense of being lost, foolish, and almost betrayed. An area he championed to knew so well and couldn't imagine acting this way.

He made it to the bathroom, and it was indeed unlocked. No highway patrol worker was making their way up through all this precipitation mayhem just to lock a bathroom that no one in their right mind would seek out. The room was so cold that James had to give himself a pep talk beforehand. It was so numbingly cold in the mountain pass restroom that he thought about Ivan Denisovich and quickly surmised that he would never be cut out for a work camp in Siberia.

He prepped himself for the cold and hustled out the door. He quickly located his car and with his arms and chin buried into his chest, he made his way through the tundra. The sounds of idling engines went in and out of his ears and the wind picked up and died down.

Halfway back to his car, he noticed a car that had no lights on and what looked like no motor running.

Peculiar.

In five steps, he managed to paint a picture of the possibilities that lay in that car. The car was an older Buick, the thing looked like a pavement boat. His grandparents had had one, which made him think the person in there could have been frozen to death. He worried about what he could see. But what if they were only half frozen? He couldn't just let them get to three-quarters frozen, and then nine-tenths frozen, and then totally frozen. At the last second, he veered toward the car and double-timed his pace.

As he approached the white car, with white rims, and white tires he noticed that it looked like someone had tried to start a message in the window. He knocked on the window carefully but urgently.

No response.

He cupped his hand up against the window and peered inside. He noticed someone was slumped in the car – their head turned slowly toward the window.

"DO YOU NEED HELP?!" James bellowed into the window, not knowing how well his voice would contend against the heavy wind.

Small movements in the car did not give James the absolute answer he was looking for. In a small break in the wind, he heard something like a lever thump below him. And then again.

Whoever was in there was trying to open the door, but they could not. It was frozen shut. This was the best guess that James had. He decided to act on his instincts and open the car door, an action that was going to be welcomed or seen as an insane time to commit grand theft auto.

With all his might he yanked on the Buick's handle. Incorrectly anticipating how frozen shut the door was, he nearly ripped the door off its old hinges. Stumbling backward into a pile of snow, he immediately questioned how wet he had just gotten and how consequential that would be soon after. Slipping like a Saturday morning cartoon cat on a greased-up kitchen floor, James felt like a fool who had made the situation worse for whoever was on the other side of that door. Any heat they did have, was surely gone. Finally regaining his balance, he moved quickly to the open door.

Inside was a diminutive, elderly woman, whether she was small from genetics or small because she had shrunk from the cold was up for debate. What he could tell instantly was that the car didn't have any source of heat in it for a couple of hours, at least. Her hands were up near her face, trying to capture every morsel of heat that she expelled with each breath. Her eyes tracked up toward James, but her head did not move. He had no idea what this meant from a physiological point, or if it meant anything at all, but the look was despair. "Ah, jeez. We gotta get you out of here." James scrambled across the scared woman to try and find the best handle to escort and extract this frozen body from the old bucket seat.

As he worked to get her out, he conferred with her about the steps he was taking, a simple way to let her know that he was on her side. As he was working, he realized that was getting colder, a piece of information that he had forgotten about because he was working himself into a sweat.

James was never actually sure how close to being frozen alive the woman was, she may have been just fine or could have been minutes away from an icy grave. It wasn't anything he pontificated on in the moment or after. He worked quickly and methodically to try and help. "I am going to bring you to my car – it's warm there. Okay?" James negotiated with the woman, but he certainly felt like he had the high position. She barely nodded.

At no point did he think about asking if there was anything she needed in the car, if there was something, he could make the haul over afterward. This was a much more dangerous situation for one of them, but James was not the victim here. He brought the woman to the passenger side of the car and ran back around to jump inside and push the door open, effectively moving some of the piled-up snow. A path now created, he hopped back out and moved around the car like it was a rainy spring day – quickly and trying to avoid the thick drops of Pacific Northwest rain.

All The Things That Could Be

Gently, he navigated the stranger into the cab and shut the door. He walked back around to the driver's side door and wonkily plopped into the seat. The heater had been running high, but in all the excitement he forgot about the assorted punk playlist that was assaulting the speakers and now this woman's ears. When he looked at her and apologized before turning down the raucous Minor Threat song which thrashed on, she looked unphased by the music. She was focused on the warmth, and she may have been unsure if the heat was generated by the dashboard or the music, either way, she did not want to offend either and risk it being taken away from her.

James lied when he rubbed his hands together and blew into them, indicating his body temperature was uncomfortably low. At that moment, he read the woman and decided that was what she needed to see – he was cold, and it was okay that she was too. She stared through the windshield, or rather at it as there was nothing but white upon it. Eventually, the look of inflexibility and of having seen too much in war melted away, and she started to slowly morph back into a human.

"Thank you. I thought...that was going to be it." She spoke and James looked forward, completely aloof as to what the correct response was to the admission. He could not imagine being stuck in a car on a routine trip, presumably she was, and being buried to the point of believing that there were mere hours, or minutes, to live. After that sobering thought crossed his mind, he fumbled out, "Ah yeah. No problem. I am glad I could help."

He felt like that couldn't be the end of his turn to speak, it would have been awkward and incomplete, so he pushed on. "What happened? Why didn't you turn your car on, you were about to freeze to death." Pointing out the obvious so well that he should have been awarded a Boy Scout badge to prove how well he could do it.

"I had my car on, it was on all night. But I drifted off to sleep and when I awoke, I could not start the car again."

James' knowledge was truly limited when it came to automobiles. A skill that he never cared too much to learn about, a decision he was currently regretting. With his novice knowledge of cars, he guessed it was either that it ran out of gas or, maybe, an alternator. He would not have bet the house on either of those guesses.

They finally introduced one another. The woman was Carol.

Understanding that the next couple of questions could be a bit sensitive, James chose his words carefully and presented them tenderly – not wanting the woman to feel incompetent. But before he opened his mouth to ask, he decided against it. Anything he asked would be further thinly veiled with "Did you not want to survive? Were you okay just dying in there?" His first question was already not well thought out, no need to go for redemption and risk further humiliation.

Instead, James pried about things that were innocuous and only related to why they were stuck in that car together.

"I am on my way over to see my grandson's graduation." People were waiting for Carol and there were people unsure of her status and may believe she was lost.

"Would you like to call someone on my phone? Let them know where you are. If there is reception, that is." James began to reach for his phone at the bottom center console and fished for the one device he promised not to use.

"I don't know the number."

"I could go and get your phone."

"I do not have one."

James looked forward and felt a secondhand worry for her family members, which he felt funny about because he knew that she was safe, and he could ensure that she got out of that storm safe and sound. A surge of purpose and sense coursed through his veins.

"I can be helpful." He thought and smiled in his head.

All The Things That Could Be

The unlikely duo sat together and ate food that James had packed for his trip. With each passing hour, each bite of food, each light-hearted piece of conversation that was had, James knew that Carol was going to see that graduation (she had allotted a couple of days for visiting before the ceremony). The radio's monotonous voice informed them that the plows were out, and the weather was changing. Like the wild weather patterns of ice and cold that swept into the pass, so did the warm and the sun.

There was nothing to do but sit and wait. They flipped through the channels of the radio and listened to old labor songs from one of the local channels. Carol seemed to have a connection to each of the songs that came up, and James felt like he was living in a modern history lesson. Her father, like his before him, was a longtime union man – one who continued the fight that the other had started. Both of them loved old Joe Hill songs.

As the weather continued to change, their spirits began to lift. The attitude within the car had lightened significantly, her face saw less of her age attached to it. Joe Hill and his Wobbly message became more and more clear as the light penetrated the windshield. Plows rumbled by and James watched trucks start to leave the parking lot. The exodus had begun. They were free. He felt relief but then felt like maybe he was being dramatic.

All The Things That Could Be

He knew he would've been fine but felt unsure about Carol's fate if he had not intervened. Saved a life? Seemed like a stretch. But she looked like she was in a bit of trouble.

He didn't think much more about it. He had helped, and Carol was thankful.

Checking out the car, he realized that she had just run out of gas – she must have shown up to the pass with the light on. Luckily, there was a gas station very nearby.

He took Carol and a gas can to the nearby station and got her all squared away.

Saying their goodbyes didn't take too long. Carol took the time to thank him and got teary-eyed about it. He felt almost uncomfortable at the praise, he didn't feel like he had earned it. As she heaped the praise on him, a sense of imposter syndrome draped him. She made him seem like a hero.

He wasn't a hero. He was just a guy.

All The Things That Could Be

10

Picking up and moving on. Sometimes you get these curveballs thrown at you and you swing and miss. This happens for a couple of different reasons. Perhaps, you've never seen a curveball before and when that sucker breaks off, you didn't think it was possible that a human could command such sorcery on an object. The ball isn't where it was supposed to be, but your bat is. Unfortunately for you, just because something is supposed to be at a certain place at a certain time, does not mean it is so. It may not seem fair, but you're just not familiar with what all humans are capable of.

Alternatively, you do know what is coming. The guy tips his pitches. But you never practice hitting off-speed pitches. They baffle you and buckle you. So, when that pitch is on its way and you know it's going to fall off the table, you swing, but to no avail. Then there are the lucky few, they have never heard of baseball, no idea who Uncle Charley is, and they hit a 450-foot dinger through the marine layer with nothing but a pool noodle.

Opportunity comes whether you are ready for it or not. Some people can adapt in the moment, even if they are ill-prepared. Some cannot. We do not always get to choose the times when opportunities approach us, and I have been guilty of squandering opportunities. But with time and failure comes understanding. It can be a tough lesson that no one wants to learn the hard way, but sometimes that is the way it goes.

I was lucky to be in the right place at the right time. I was lucky that I had the opportunity to help someone who needed it. How

All The Things That Could Be

many times have I wasted the chance though? Is my journey an opportunity or running away from one? Maybe, this is me taking the easy way out of having to confront my opportunities at home. Maybe, I will find some answers to that question soon.

Who am I – the person who gets fooled by the curveball because I have never seen it, or the person who knows it is coming but refuses to prepare for it – so I am content with failure because the excuse I have is "I could do that, but I simply do not want to. The effort required to put in, I would rather exert somewhere else." I'm not lazy, I just don't care – a convenient excuse. Only those who use it will believe it from others, and that is out of solidarity and to validate themselves when they say it.

Like MFDOOM said in his sage-like wisdom, "Time waits for no man." I guess that means me, too.

-JD

11

The rain punished the road which was a stark reminder that he was no longer in the bosom of the Pacific Northwest where the weather wasn't as direct and rude. With his map on the seat next to him, sprawled out in a codified way that only he would understand, the AM radio buzzed on gently. Old tunes crackled throughout the car, songs about working-class heroes and a labor struggle – songs about a war seemingly lost decades ago but the hymns of rebellion marched on, maybe they would reach the right ears and the battle would recommence, maybe one day AM radio would go away and so would the movement.

The highway was empty and there had not been a sign indicating his preferred speed for what seemed like thousands of miles, minutes, seconds, or songs – time had become different in the car. Days were shorter and longer, nights the same. He knew that not too much time had passed, however, because he was still turning down the radio to see better in the rain.

The windshield wipers chased one another fervently but never got any closer – an eternal game of tag until they would one day find themselves in a landfill, their replacements ready to continue their legacy. However futile the game was, they worked hard to do the best they could.

As he crept toward civilization, bridges were indicators, he started to look for some blue signs indicating

All The Things That Could Be

food and sleep. Food in the form of restaurants and sleep in the form of a parking lot. In his mind, he was already ordering and imagining the layout of his car – a sleeping situation that was proving not as bad as he was warned against. Some nights were tougher than others, but that was the fault of the temperature. Some nights he was stretched out, others he was completely spherical.

An overpass in the distance was made visible as the clouds declined to further bless the land. The man and machine were moving forward toward darkness and the night would soon envelop the sky. A strange light flashed sporadically under the bridge.

A message perhaps.

Morse Code?

James didn't know Morse Code to begin with, but he quickly ruled it out. While there wasn't a complex message being beamed to him, he noticed that there was someone, or something, trying to get his attention. With no cars in front of him or behind him for as far as he could see (far enough to matter), he slowed down as he approached the light. Alien abduction? Maybe. Maybe not. What an adventure that would be.

His eyes tried to guess what he was going to see, but what was there came into focus quickly. A bedraggled man, carrying a backpack. His face was streaked with dirt and filth, with jutting facial features that saw his skin wrapping tight around the peaks and valleys of his face. He smiled and used one hand to wave down the car – an expression of hope and surprise covered his less-than-hopeful appearance. Based on the motion and body language, James guessed he had been at this for a while.

In his mind, he thought that if he drove away, it was a victimless crime. He was not expected to take orders from this man who used some lightwork trickery to seduce a potential victim. They were both in the middle of nowhere, using a western Washington metric, but on the outskirts of a metropolis by Montana ones.

James had never picked up a hitchhiker and didn't know anyone who had. Picking them up was like signing your death warrant, at least that is what had been sold to many people. "If I drive by, he will never care. He would just see me as another in the mass of suspects who never wanted to take the chance." James said quietly to his steering wheel.

He felt his car start to slow and pull to the side. He wasn't sure if he was the cause of these two uncharacteristic movements or not, but he did know that the car was about to open and let this stranger in.

The car stopped and the man let out a "Ha!" and scurried over to the passenger side.

The window rolled down and James quickly formulated everything that he was going to say for the rest of the journey. However, when his mouth opened, he forgot the entire script. Like a middle school student in their debut play: scene one, act one. Silence.

The man's wrinkled flannel was covered by a jacket that was never meant to go with the shirt. It was no surprise upon first looking at this man that he took what he could get, and no complaints would be registered from him. It was tough to figure out exactly what kind of jeans he was wearing – whether they were beat up by design or tough times. They were too short and dark socks worked as a transition to his shoes that looked like shoes from any mall in America.

He looked like he smelled, but also looked like he was prone to emotion. He looked like he hadn't made an honest dollar for a while. He also looked like he once had dreams as a child.

An awkward pause lingered in the air as the two men stared back at each other. James could feel the air blowing in his face while the mysterious stranger felt the welcomed heat. Not wanting to be presumptuous and ruin any opportunity to potentially crawl into a warm front seat, he didn't say anything. James fumbled out a response that would have been comical in most settings, "What's up?"

"Uh, not too much. Just trying to get to Deer Lodge."

"Deer Lodge? You're a way out from Deer Lodge." James had done a fine job of studying his map and knew towns that even state residents were unaware of.

"Yeah, well, that is why I am tired of walking and need a ride."

James felt silly at the obvious comment. He didn't want to come off as foolish, he felt like it would increase any thoughts of nefarious ideas held by the man. He could still punch it and get out alive and unscathed. A victimless crime on humanity. Kind of.

He rolled through all the possibilities and the percentage chance in which this would end his adventure. Counterpoint – this made it a more adventurous adventure.

"Alright man, get on in." James smiled and rolled up the window while unlocking the door. Smiling would show friendliness – an ally worth sparing.

He shuffled into the seat and placed his backpack of many things into the backseat. He swung back around, so quickly that it made James duck to avoid the sure blow that was going to cave in his skull.

He felt an immediate pain radiate throughout his head as he headbutted his steering wheel.

"Jeez, are you okay, dude?" the new traveler stopped his motion altogether to check in on his new ally.

"Yeah, just…" James couldn't find the words to bail him out of suggesting that he perceived this person he picked up as a serial killer. "Yeah, I'm good. I don't know what happened." He rubbed his head and eventually, the pain subsided to a dull ache.

"Name's Dom." He held out his gloved hand to shake with James. James reciprocated the gesture. So far, so good.

"James. So, Deer Lodge? Got some time before Deer Lodge."

"Yeah. I really appreciate the help. Been out there a while."

James realized that this adventure had an opportunity for him to glean knowledge on something he had no idea about. He felt as if he were joining a trade in something he had never even considered. He put the car into drive and began to pull back on the road.

"How long do you hitchhike for before you get picked up, usually? Something you do often? Certainly, some stigma that goes along with it. Do you ever get worried about who picks you up?" Unpolished, James shotgunned questions to Dom, loading him up with a lot to think about and the perceptions of those who don't need to ask for rides about those who rely on them.

"Depends on the day and the place. Out here, you may be waiting a while but that is also because you go so long without seeing anyone. Lately, I have had to rely more on it. Haven't denied someone yet but haven't done this for too long." He turned the questions into answers and put them right back on James.

Dom and James drove for a half-hour and the conversation became quite easy. James told Dom of his adventure and Dom was intrigued by it. He also thought it was a bit foolish, but he didn't let on. Some of that came from jealousy: here was someone who had things figured out and going well for them, and they threw it away because they were bored. Dom saw it as a luxury he would like to have but one that was not, and never had been, afforded to him.

12

Dom grew up in eastern Montana and had never strayed too far from the state. He grew up with two brothers and all of them lived together with their mother, who worked full-time to put food on the table. The brothers had to take care of each other and that sometimes meant they found the same trouble all together. All of them were separated by four years total, Dom being the middle. When the oldest brother found their mother's cigarettes in her room and brought three out, they all decided to try this thing their mother had forbidden but also was rarely seen without. They took a simultaneous drag, and all began to hack, cough, and gag – the neophyte smoker's holy trinity.

When their mom got home, she already knew what had happened. She could smell the smoke and knew exactly how many cigarettes were in her pack before she left for work. The windows were open in the middle of February and there was a new burn mark in the couch. She lined all the boys up on the couch and gave them hell with a belt.

"Get your butts to bed." Dom was the most sensitive of the three and turned around. He stood there yearning for an embrace of his mother to remind him that even in mistakes there was grace. She motioned for him to get to bed, and his head drooped. He turned around and slowly waddled back to his room, rubbing his butt where the leather bit him over and over.

All The Things That Could Be

No one ever spoke of Dominque Haywood in hushed tones, and they never put his name in the same sentence as "Ivy League Education". But they never put his name in the same sentence as "sociopath" or "murderer". Mainly because no one spoke his name much, ever. When he dropped out at sixteen, his missing quiet presence in his school was hardly noticed. An average student, with an average voice, who did and said average things – they are forgotten the quickest.

The Haywoods lived in Scobey, Montana – a place so small that it may or may not have been real. Dom's dad passed away or ran away when he was little. The story his mother told never made sense to him, but he never questioned her. He had done some small amount of sleuthing on his own, enough to confirm his suspicions correctly. He never pushed further than that, whether his dad was dead or with another family, or no family, or many families, was irrelevant. He was gone.

Growing up, Dom never said "This is tough" or "This is easy" regarding his family's living situation because it just *was*. He didn't know any other way, but he did know that his mom was often tired, short, and sad. He often witnessed her frustrated. He assumed it was toward the boys, but it wasn't until she was in a high-pitched fever dream that she had been teleported back in time and while sweating profusely and still asleep, she confessed to someone that "I just wanted better for the boys." This was often Dom's last thought before he punished himself with a belt.

All The Things That Could Be

Poverty ensured the family struggled mightily; it worked as a shield to keep money away from them. Like an Iron Dome against prosperity, any time money came towards the household, it was immediately used to pay a bill or someone. Dom and his brothers got jobs as soon as they could to help provide. But bad went to worse when mother got sick. Dom dropped out of high school to turn a part-time job into a full-time misery. He got on at the local tire shop, a dead-end position that paid not nearly enough to support the family adequately, but enough that he could say he was doing something. Dom spread out his tentacles all over town to find better work, pay, and mobility – but he was handcuffed by circumstances. His tentacles had a small radius – a subject he just started learning about in high school before he left.

He quickly realized that the world was no longer for the poor, and he couldn't be sure, but he didn't think it ever was. Little education translated to little hope – if people only knew why he gave up his opportunity, they may feel inclined to bless him with another. But businesses care about what you have, not what you might have with a little work. Without any schooling, he knew he would need three times the work experience and ten times the luck of someone who stuck it out.

Modern-day panhandling was begging his boss for another fifty-cent raise, something that would quickly be rendered useless by rising costs. He wasn't sure, but Dom sometimes believed that prices were directly linked to how much money he was making. Sometimes, he believed, that if he stopped working, then everyone would live better and pay less. When he eventually did stop working, he found out it wasn't the case.

He never planned to start slamming heroin. No one ever wakes up one day and says, "I want to inject my veins with heroin for the first time today."

Whether people dream of waking up with a syringe in their arm and a belt threatening to cut off blood supply to their extremities or not, these things happen. They happened to a lot of people, and they happened to Dom.

He had been a heavy user for five years (one and a half in addict years). Like James, he had sold many things to ensure he could continue his journey for as long as possible. He was on a journey that had no distinct end destination. Odds are, he would end up broke, miserable, and dead – probably in that order. There was a small chance that "recovered" would be a destination.

Dom had moments of sobriety, however. Those were painful. Those breaks happened because he had no goods to sell and no dope to slam. Involuntary sobriety. But plenty of sobriety starts that way. In his mind, he was on his way to eventual recovery. Somewhere in the far reaches of his mind, he was already fixed.

This son of three and brother to two was currently on one of those sober streaks, but it wasn't anything he was celebrating. He was actively looking for a way to break that streak, as he had recently come across some pilfered goods and was able to make some cash. He had a connection, Big Barry, who had supplied him for the last couple of years. The prices rarely went up, but the need to purchase more always did. Big Barry, whose first name, Dom thought, probably wasn't Big, but Barry, also told him to be careful and not to do too much. Dom saw this as a caring gesture when it was Big Barry wanting to keep his clientele coming back for more. Big Barry didn't make money from guys who were underground.

Make them be zombies, which is fine. Keep them as zombies, that's preferable. However, keeping them alive and addicted, that's most important.

There was a problem: distance. Dom was in Missoula and needed to travel quite a long way to get to Deer Lodge. Big Barry ran a lucrative business right next to the best buyers: the Deer Lodge Prison. If he ever got caught, he may not have to travel too far to his new home. He was confident he could still run his business from the inside, he had done it before.

A storm was coming, but it in no way dissuaded Dom from making the journey. His addict personality was persistent – you had to admire that. He may have been sober, but he would do whatever he had to get a fix. If he was as dogged at anything productive in life as he was about getting smack, he wouldn't be in the position he was in. But there was nothing else out there that he had yet found, which had the same draw to make him work to get it.

Missoula was the land of opportunity. There were so many commuters, and each one was an opportunity to get him to his land of milk and honey. He anticipated he would need to wait an hour or so to finally get someone to stop, but it was better than other places he had been.

His best handwriting, smile, and wave would eventually net him a ride with an older couple. They reminded him of his grandparents and part of him dreaded getting a ride to get hard drugs from his grandparents – or people who reminded him of them. He was grateful for the ride, and they took him to Clinton and the small talk was minimal. His hosts were hard of hearing and at some point, he thinks they turned off their hearing aids to mute the awkward silence.

Being dropped off in Clinton was a blessing and a curse. A blessing because he was that much closer to his goal, a curse because finding a ride out of Clinton would be tough. He thanked the couple and unloaded his goods. The woman in the passenger seat looked at her watch and warned him that it was going to be dark soon while digging through the glove compartment. She pulled out a small flashlight and handed it to Dom. "This is very kind of you. Thank you." Dom shut the door; she rolled down the window. "Be safe out there." Safe was a relative term.

All The Things That Could Be

He did the math in his head – junkie math. "How many cars are there in the town? How likely are they to give me a ride? If I started walking now, would it be better to simply flag down people as I went?" Like a calculator, the math was done quickly. Unlike a calculator, he might be wrong. He began to walk.

Cars traveling down I-90 went fast, sometimes very fast. It wasn't that long ago that Montana had no speed limits at all, and out of a willingness to stick it to the man, or a desire to see a friend five minutes sooner, many drivers treated the speed limit signs as foreign suggestions. This brought potential problems to junkies who were walking (sometimes stumbling) down the road.

Montana roads were often empty, on account that the population was small – Dom thought this funny since the state was so big and so beautiful. The scenes in western Montana would have rivaled any state's best views. So beautiful, so serene, so calm. Lots of nukes, though. Ready at any moment to end the world. Life was sometimes like that though.

He tried his best to make eye contact as people zipped by – most drivers didn't even look at him. He had ditched his sign in Clinton – there was no question as to what a thumbs up meant by a scraggly guy with a beat-up backpack on the side of a highway meant. As he walked toward the high he longed for, he saw the storm was almost upon him.

All The Things That Could Be

His Montana senses told him that within fifteen minutes, he was going to be in trouble. He quickened his pace.

On this long walk, he got to be alone with his thoughts – outside of the high, this was one of his favorite parts about being a junkie: quiet, highway walking, a time to think about life. Sometimes thinking about life was profound and encouraging – maybe he didn't need the drugs he sought. Maybe he could clean up, become something, go back to school, get a good job, and have a nice family. The pull of these ideas was always stronger than the previous time he had them, maybe one day he could see it through. But until then, he would walk. Maybe, he thought, being a junkie will bring me to get my life right one day.

Clouds moving closer. Lightning strikes in the distance. A wall of rain approaching. His time as a dry man was coming to an end unless he could quickly find a solution. His eyes scanned the horizon for possible solutions – he had not been doing I-90 enough to remember exactly what was where – so he searched. A small overpass on the horizon was a haven for him and a possible resting spot for the night. He couldn't continue his journey in the rain and dark. He knew his lifestyle was risky, but this seemed like an unnecessary risk. Better to camp for the night in the dry. At the very least, he knew he wouldn't be bothered.

By the time he reached the underside of the overpass, the rain had just started to come down, lightly at first, biblical next. He meandered to the other side of the underpass and saw that the rain would break before too long, but there seemed to be more on the way. Darkness coupled with the storm and rolled in quickly. Dom went back to the original entrance and got his flashlight out. Three or four cars came through in the next half-hour but none of them paid him much mind.

As the rain pounded the pavement and thunder ripped through the sky, headlines appeared in view. Dom acted like a strung-out Airport Marshall with his flashlight. Any UFOs in the area would have been skeptical about the message being sent by this. He made grand, sweeping gestures – pointing his flashlight everywhere but directly into the eyes of the driver. He didn't want to ruin his chances.

And then, a miracle. The car began to slow down. This person may *actually* stop.

The car rolled to a stop under the bridge. He let out a laugh, but not because anything was funny. Dom was shocked and mentally prepared for the cruelty of the person driving away after building up his hope. The window rolled down and the man inside just stared at him. He wasn't sure if he was part of some joke right now because the silence between the two went on for a long time. Two modern-day western gunfighters – each ready to pull a greeting out of their holster. The stranger beat him to the draw.

"What's up?"

13

James didn't try to pry much information regarding why or where Dom was going. Partially this was out of respect for his own business and out of fear of knowing the answer. Dom rolled up his sleeves to reveal a map of poor tattoos and track marks. If he were using, he didn't seem high right now. Waldo would be impressed.

Extreme curiosity gripped James and questions about what compelled this person to jam a needle into his veins and inject some poison. He knew that he couldn't be too forward, so he started at the genesis.

Dom was gracious and gave him the abridged, but those parts were an unregulated, version of his life. What was the point in not telling the truth? His appearance left little to the imagination as to how his days shook out, he saw it in the disgusted faces of the people who passed him daily and acted like he was invisible except only to let him know they highly disapproved of who they thought he was. Sometimes he laughed, he knew that if he was part of their families, how their looks of disgust would change to looks of sadness and empathy. "He fell on hard times. He really is a good kid. He has been through a lot. When he gets clean, he is going to do great things."

After his mother died and his brothers began a Haywood diaspora (small, but still counts), Dom was only twenty and impressionable. His impressionability mixed with depression made a cocktail that was so glamorous and self-destructive that it made scientists and social workers gasp with wonder and disbelief. Like a Maryland Heights nightmare scenario, the underground fire finally met the nuclear waste, and the results were phenomenal.

One brother moved to Boston and the other to Drummond, dangerously close to Deer Lodge in Montana miles. His contact with them was spotty as best, his brothers were aware of his habits and started to develop an idea that Dom's desire to stay fraternal was transactional.

For a few years, whenever his brothers got a text message or phone call from Dom, his "hello" was translated to "I need money." It was unfair to Dom because he no longer asked, he cursed the junkie community for it. He worked to assuage those fears by keeping in better communication and asking about them and their families. Never bringing up money, never bringing up himself. They would occasionally ask, and he would usually respond with "same ol', same ol'" which was code for "still struggling". Over time, their guards were lowered, and they no longer felt pre-emptively resentful of messages. Just pity, sadness, and a tinge of nostalgia.

Almost overnight, Dom had a magnet to many self-destructive behaviors. Many of them worked as a team, one behavior assisting bringing in another, more destructive behavior. A leveled-up behavior, not just one that you start with, but one you need to work on to achieve. The higher the level they are, the harder they are to defeat. Life sometimes felt like a game. Sometimes that game was fun and sometimes that game was not.

Hanging out with people involved in bad things (he avoided using the term bad people because he realized they were all kids duped by instant gratification) led to him being involved in bad things. At first, it started with OxyContin, but Oxy started to not be enough and it cost too much to stay feeling normal. The thieving had begun, the panhandling, the misery. But the skies parted, and the sun came out when the heroin arrived. This was a great financial move by Dom. He would now be saving money and getting a better high than before. Maybe one day when he was clean, he would study economics.

He never made a serious attempt at quitting – the ups, historically, outweighed the downs and he didn't feel the need to alter the natural order of his universe. If this wasn't supposed to be this good, then it wouldn't be – a rationalization he often stuck by.

The lifestyle became one of self-manipulation and mental gymnastics in some ways.

He misattributed thieving to natural selection.

Friends who died just took too much. Natural selection.

Doing a few jailhouse stints? Dry sleep, warm meals. Natural selection.

All The Things That Could Be

The fact of the matter was he was staying alive. Survival was key. Just had to keep surviving until the next cloud break. Until the next sunshine.

Skies weren't as clear as they once were.

He was trying to hold on to those days, trying to handle cumulonimbi and keep them from amassing in protest of his foolish ways, attempting to reach beyond the horizon and pull the sun from its locality to take over the moon's job...not easy.

See current situation: bumming rides and trying to race a storm to a bridge, hoping that another bummed ride will present itself. And your reward? Travel to a prison town to buy one of the most self-destructive substances that money can buy. It will cost you money and could cost you your life.

James felt sad for Dom. He felt empathy. He felt connection. He understood the feeling of the journey they were both on. Neither one of them had an outcome they were willing to try and predict, both of their journeys could fall flat on their faces. While James had never dealt with the issue of addiction, he had dealt with the predecessor – sadness and grief. When the fork in the road came, they both just chose different paths. Now their paths ran parallel to one another.

The answer to the next question was one that James braced for, "so what's in Deer Lodge for you?"

All The Things That Could Be

"Old habits." It was a risky confession, but he also felt the need to be straight with the person who gave him transport. He felt like this driver could handle the truth and would not judge him too harshly. He had already got mileage covered, if he did need to find another car, he would be okay with it. The realization was unusual in that he felt his gratitude overpower his desire for using. Maybe he was getting sober.

In the depths of their conversation, the warm car decided it, too, yearned for something that it needed to keep going, as a little, orange light illuminated the dashboard. James had been aware of it when he picked up Dom but knew there were enough places between there and Helena to be safe. "Gotta get some gas." James let it be known well before the exit came so as not to make the passenger feel his story had ruined the opportunity for the full ride. In the back of his mind, and he hated to admit it, he didn't want to awaken any potential volatility by suggesting he might be abandoning this person immediately after a voluntary dashboard confessional.

The rain had picked back up, pattering the hood of the car gently. Unbeknownst to either one of them, it was one of the other's favorite sounds. Pulling into the pumps, James always had to look and see what way the arrow was pointing, indicating where the fuel tank was. He could drive the same car for forty years, and he would still need to look.

All The Things That Could Be

Putting it into the park, James pulled up on the emergency brake out of habit. Even being on flat ground, some sort of superstition made him always make sure the emergency brake was on. It may have been silly, but it comforted him.

Dom got his backpack out of the backseat – if James decided to leave him (he didn't think he would) it would have been devastating to lose everything he owned in that backpack. It only took him one time to find out: you always keep your possessions with you. He slung it over his shoulder, and, like a well-choreographed act, his other arm went right between the other strap and the pack. He didn't need to think about the action, like a professional baseball player, who could put a ninety-five miles per hour fastball between the second and third eye of a tarantula from sixty feet six inches away. Also, that's a quick death.

The two journeying adventurers walked into the store, crossing from a threshold of cold and dark to a fluorescent glow – the light and heat may have been manufactured, but it felt nice compared to the outside. A bearded man with suspenders trapping a red, tucked-in flannel against his body stood behind the counter, he looked like he may not have moved for a couple of days, except for the slow head turn as they passed his commercial threshold.

"Evenin'."

James and Dom nodded at the clerk and moved toward the bathroom – both men in need of the same thing:

All The Things That Could Be

relief and a snack. James was sure he was getting one, but Dom was not. James was sure Dom was getting one, however – he couldn't deny him something so easy. He hadn't known hunger like Dom had, and while James wasn't completely familiar with the level, he assumed. He felt it inhumane to deny helping curb the painful sensation, were it present.

James washed his hands and opened the door into the hallway which led back into the store. A commotion rang out. Muffled at first but then it became very clear. Dom almost ran right into James' back, but he shushed him and held out his hand to make what he hoped would be an impassable barrier. Dom froze in his footsteps and keyed into the commotion in the store.

The duo crept closer.

"Smokes! Money! Wallet! Now!" a muffled voice rang out. This was meant to be quick and easy. Smash and grab. Bingo, bango, bongo. Get in, get money, get out.

James started to move down the hall, risking coming out into the store and becoming a victim. Dom made a near-silent noise to get his attention, James turned around and motioned Dom to stay put. The transient man mouthed "What the hell are you doing?" and James couldn't answer – but he was doing something.

What is an adventure without a little danger? This wasn't an endeavor that James would have embarked on

All The Things That Could Be

before. Historically, he had been afraid to die – he knew the pain it left. "On the other hand," he thought, "I gotta see this."

He peaked around the corner to see the clerk with his hands in the air and his face as red as his shirt. He looked like he was sweating, or crying, it was tough to tell. The accosting party had a gun pointed at the man's face, a car parked wonky and still running outside – an unknowing accomplice – ready to ruin someone's day. Did the car even consider that it was engaged in criminal activity? If it were aware, would it have shut off? Or drove the nefarious man to the police station? To his house? Off a cliff?

James ducked down and squat-walked through an aisle – he knew he would feel this in the morning. He slinked through the aisle as the man continued to bark out orders. His understanding of the situation was the clerk was too scared to move despite the very direct instructions while facing down the barrel of a gun.

Dom felt like he needed to go and observe the situation, if for no other reason than there is strength in numbers. Was James going to overpower the guy? Talk him down? Try and get a cut of the loot? He crept down the hall, like Christmas morning when he was eleven – can't wake mom.

The thief's voice was pointed away from Dom, this much he knew. Slowly, barely, cautiously, he moved his eye around the corner. He saw James haunting slowly, squatting so low that Dom felt like his own quads were destined to snap.

If Dom believed in luck, it changed in that moment. Being abandoned was not something that was new to him, but it was usually in the form of people. Certainly, he often was an active contributor as to why those people left him, but he knew abandonment all the same. Yet, it was something very different to be abandoned by something material. In that moment, Dom would have begged for abandonment if he only knew the betrayal that he received instead.

The backpack which had served him so faithfully in his darkest hours had, in the most inopportune moment, turned into the loudest ping on the most dangerous sonar. In a millisecond he went from a stealthy submarine in the sea to a bumbling oil tanker floating lifelessly into port after being on fire for the last eight hours.

Whipping around, gun first, the assailant spotted Dom and hauled off toward him. The gas station convenience store was Montana big – multiple rows, a small supermarket. Leaving the traitor carrying receptacle to die if it must, the wanderer, perhaps soon to be wandering another world, scurried on his hands and knees to the soda machine – the opposite way from James.

"You call the cops, or you move a muscle, I will find your family!" The robber waved a wallet, belonging to the cashier.

All The Things That Could Be

James looked through the perforated shelves and got the location of the man. His best view yet, he saw this wasn't his first job: sunglasses (in a storm at night?), a kerchief concealing the rest of his face, bland and black clothing with no distinguished markings, white gloves – one which contrasted perfectly with the black handle of the pistol. A picture deserving of the Louvre, this man was an artist. A broken and tattered backpack, which left Laos dark purple, marked a crime scene – art. The entire convenience store: a story that belonged to be studied in the annals of art history.

Hiding behind an end cap, James watched the hunter. The hunter had no idea that he was potentially prey, in the right circumstance. He mulled around violently, thrashing and inflicting fear throughout the four corners and holding that small part of Montana hostage – unbeknownst to more than seven billion people on planet Earth. The convenience store was the gladiatorial arena for four people. Again, believers of Descartes knew that for four people, the entire world, universe, and existence itself hung in the balance.

The predator looked feverishly for his prey, but James began to stalk him. An otherwise docile man, he never sought violence and was quite against it. In the same breath, he understood that sometimes survival required it, as a lock required a key.

What would happen if he met the thief? He had to think.

All The Things That Could Be

Dom scurried down the row two aisles over, hoisting James back into reality.

Dom was now a slow-moving American consumer ship in the open Atlantic in 1942. He was tracked. Too slow to escape, too stiff to outmaneuver.

James ran to the other end of the aisle, if he wasn't careful, he would run directly into the gunman. He heard him turn the corner into Dom's aisle, who was doing all he could to get out of the area, which was putting himself in a crabwalk position, but he kept slipping. He was caught.

"Give me your wallet and your cash. Let's go." A gun barrel demanded of the man who had neither.

A stammering and shocked Dom tried to explain an entire lifestyle of poverty living in stuttering syllables. The gun demanded faster, better, more expensive answers.

Continuing to crab-walk backward, a completely futile act now, as the gunman was walking over him, Dom finally knocked his head on the freezer – if the glass were not present, he would have backed right into some off-brand waffles. "Poor. Homeless." Was all he was able to get out, in a last-ditch attempt he rolled up his sleeves to show the tracks from the drug use.

"Well, no one will care then." The gun cocked.

James Dalley sometimes thought about what he would do when faced with death. Now, admittedly, he could

All The Things That Could Be

have bolted out of that store right then and been spared. He could have run past the clerk who was paralyzed with fear of his own life, but also the lives of whoever was on the other end of the address on his driver's license, which the predator held in his hand and held him hostage with.

As a connoisseur of weird stories, James remembered the name "Randy Johnson". It was reported that Randy Johnson slept with a sack of baseballs near his bed. If someone ever wanted to take their chances at pilfering The Big Unit's home, the sack of balls would be the weapons of choice. Even if Randy Johnson only got three throws off, you could bet that at least one of them would meet a face or head. As soon as the foolish thief stepped inside Randy Johnson's house, he was officially a victim, he just didn't know it yet. A bird once experienced what The Big Unit could do by accident, no one wanted to experience a true Mr. Snappy that landed.

The endcap James crouched next to was his bag of baseballs. Cans of soup. Cream of chicken. He picked up a can for both hands, he would get one free shot and another, maybe. The second one would likely be not as free. He slowly walked down the aisle as the man seemingly got ready to execute the transient junkie – a true description and the only way he knew him.

Dom's eyes flickered to James, the one thing that James was hoping Dom was smart enough not to do.

Ping.

All The Things That Could Be

Recognizing the change in the direction of his eyes, the man spun around. In a second, minimizing the target, and then exposing it even more. The extended hand with the gun led the bodily shift. James reared back and was transported back to his youth – he had always loved baseball. He played for a long time and while he couldn't hit to save his life, he knew how to throw. Rather, he once knew how to throw – it had been a long time since he had.

Four-seam grip, just to make sure. Release. The body fully turned toward James. He would only get one opportunity. Good follow-through.

Dom had an opportunity to run but decided to stay for the show. He may have been too shocked to move, however.

The can screamed through the air. The arm was still swinging toward James. Impact. Glass shattered. Soup everywhere. A shot rings out. Blood and body hit the floor.

14

A hole in the ceiling would remain there for days, or years, or decades. James and Dom never know because neither of them ever returned to the shop.

The police showed up within fifteen minutes of the shot ringing out to a scene like many they had come across, except there was soup.

"That's cream of chicken. No doubt."

"Not cream of mushroom?"

"No sarge, that's chicken."

The police got the report from the victims there as they hauled away the shooter. He had been wanted in a few states for similar crimes. He was a dangerous man. He had killed before and would have killed everyone in that store, if necessary, information told to James and Dom multiple times by multiple officers. It was like they were telling Dom, "Be happy you're alive, you probably shouldn't be."

They also pulled the security footage from the store, something that the department would watch multiple times at the station – every time another officer came in from patrol or a shift change, one of those who had seen the footage would quickly beckon them over to it, "You gotta get a load of this!" and later, "Cream of chicken!"

James looked at it one time and noted that his follow-through was excellent. He got a view at a frame-by-frame rate, allowing him to analyze all parts. He was about thirty feet away, but the object arrived at its destination very quickly. The can started to turn in midair, he knew this when he saw the gash on the gunman's forehead. He bled quite a bit. The robber was instantly unconscious except for the synapse which fired to his finger causing him to squeeze off one round into the ceiling with his then flailing arm. The can was redirected after the initial impact into the novelty ice cream freezer glass – the can exploded from the impact. There was a lot of blood and a lot of soup. Enough blood to fill a few soup cans.

Dom and James sat around like a couple of school kids after a hallway fight – just looking around and taking it in, not knowing what to do next. Dom shook James' hand a couple of times, forgetting that he had done so, and thanking him for helping. For all the times that Dom had injected himself with liquid death, he never felt so spooked from being so close to St. Peters' gate, but death is always less scary when it's on your own terms, Dom reasoned.

"Well, you guys okay? Need an ambulance? Medical?" The police officer asked the pair. James looked over the shoulder to the clerk who finally calmed down. "Uh, no, I think we are good." James looked to Dom who nodded.

"Yeah, yeah, yeah…we are good." Still spooked.

"No cuts, bumps, gunshots, soup?" The officer joked because he knew that unlikely duo was physically okay.

"Yeah, yeah, yeah...we are good." Automatic.

Most of the store was a crime scene, but the investigator wading through blood and soup, nodded to his partner to fetch the guys the chips they were after. They brought the food up to the counter and the flannelled survivor simply put up his hand and said, "I think we are square." Dom remembered his backpack, and even though he was still feeling betrayed by it, he made sure to retrieve it.

The two adventurers stepped into the car. Tom Sawyer and Huck Finn. Sam and Frodo. James and Marco.

A moment in time that had forever bound two individuals who were but strangers mere hours ago. Life is weird sometimes.

"So yeah, that was pretty crazy, man." Both passengers sat in stunned silence for a little while, comprehending the magnitude of what they just faced.

"You think that guy will live? That was a lot of blood." Dom inquired. James nodded his head slowly. He was pretty sure the gunman was going to survive. "Yeah, I mean, I think that when you get cut in that area, a ton of blood flow is common. But yeah, it looked gnarly." Resume the thousand-yard stare.

All The Things That Could Be

They pulled out of the gas station without getting any gas. James was aware, he just needed to get away from the area. He was a pretty cool and collected guy, not often rattled, but he felt this. It wasn't unexpected – any mortal would feel the intensity of the situation. And there were plenty of gas stations between where they were and where the car would quit.

As they drove and debriefed, they internalized the situation and started to process how this would impact them moving forward. James had saved a life, maybe a few, maybe his own. Who knows where his reign of terror would have ended if he got away that night. It was satisfying to think about. He didn't possess any feelings of heroism; he just did what needed to be done in the moment. He didn't harbor any feelings of regret about the damage done – whatever happened to the predator…he earned it. In his adventure, he felt like he had picked up a companion and passed the stage, a stage he didn't know he was on. This was turning into something more than he bargained for, but that also made him grin.

"A couple of exits up here is Drummond, just drop me off there." Dom insisted.

"That's still a ways from Deer Lodge, man. I don't mind taking you all the way." James reassured.

"Nah. My brother lives there. I need to go there now. Deer Lodge can wait. Maybe Deer Lodge can stop being a location on my map. This has been a lot. I need to re-evaluate." The soul searching had already begun for Dom. Would it be fleeting? No one could know. But sometimes seeds are planted without knowing when they will grow.

Seemingly, a switch had been flipped in Dom. He simply looked forward and gave what sounded like pre-packaged responses. Answers were selected before the question was known. James stopped the conversation until they reached the Drummond exit.

"Where does your brother live?"

Dom bounced back from a shell-like automaton state and told James, "Ah nah, I can't just roll up like that. Drop me off at the park, I'll get you there."

"Not that I don't think this is a better decision than Deer Lodge, I'm not one to judge, but are you going to be alright?" He was concerned about not only his perpetual state of being without a roof (among other things) but, his sobriety, his state of mind – which, at the moment, seemed the most fragile.

"This is the most sober I have been in a while. If there is ever a time, I could turn this around, I think it is now."

The comment made James smile – made him hopeful.

"But then again, you just never know with a junkie. But tonight, I am safe and sober."

All The Things That Could Be

The car rolled to a stop at the park. Dom knew it was the park, James was going on faith – it was too dark and rainy to see.

"Well man, thanks for the ride. I really appreciate it. What a night."

"What a night. Take care, Dom."

The men's hands clapped loudly, a sound still reverberating throughout time, as they shook and departed. Dom reached into the back of the car and grabbed his falling-apart backpack. The tattered backpack banged against the seats as it lurched forward. A lifelong traveling partner, they'd been through a lot together. For a long time, that backpack was a passive participant in all the decisions made by Dom. Today, it was an active one.

15

How can you pretend to understand something that you have no experience with? Is it easier to justify our actions when we act like we know the intricacies of others? I do not need to know why that person does not work, because I already know he is lazy. I do not need to know why that child blew up that classroom and swore at that teacher (which happened to me) because I already know that the child is disrespectful and spiteful. I do not need to know any more than the information I have already ascertained. And if I obtain new information, I will apply it if it fits in with what I already think. If it doesn't, I will be skeptical.

No one likes to be wrong, so much so that we tend to argue when we are wrong, even when we know we are wrong. A society built on pride and unwavering opinion. Did someone change your mind about something? You must be weak. That evidence they provided? Biased and wrong (yeah, sometimes it is).

Dom, presumably, didn't wake up one day and say "Man, I can't wait to start killing myself slowly and completely eviscerate most of my relationships." He wasn't doing this because it brought him joy, on the contrary, it brought him sorrow. He was salting a field of tulips — of course, this wasn't his preference of how to handle such floral.

If I were a betting man, I would guess the journey that got Dom from a young boy with dreams to a man begging for rides to get high was a long and arduous journey that happened on a road he didn't ever see himself traveling down. But he was on that road now and perhaps he was trying to navigate his way off of it, or maybe he wasn't.

All The Things That Could Be

Should we do better by our fellow man and assume good intent? It seems like giving the benefit of the doubt to someone who is strung out is a fool's errand. What if we took a look into the past — what would we see? Two spots on a map: one of them is over-prescribed pain medication and the other is shooting up heroin. The distance between those two points isn't as far as you might think. No one ever thinks "This could happen to me", so if that is the case then I guess it's fair to say, "If it could happen to you, it could happen to me."

We are all one or two slips away from being down the mountainside, trying to climb back up to where we fell. But the distance is long and the journey back up is slippery.

-JD

16

One of his more core memories was neither good nor bad – or at least he wasn't sure which one he would have considered it. He was driving home with his dad after school one day, the rumbling of the old truck proved that something could be frozen in time and anyone who rode in that truck was transported back in time for the duration of the ride. When you were in that truck, the year was 1979. His dad had just come from work, a simple explanation as to why he was the last kid picked up from school. His father looked tired and dirty, but his exhausted nature never broke through in the way of anger or rage. He was a patient man, he had to be. He had been laboring in the same factory for fifteen years, married to the same woman for twenty years, and cheered for the same team for forty. Patience was a known virtue to Joe Dalley. There were very few times when James saw his father rattled.

James looked out the window as he bobbed up and down from the ride. He was cozied into a vehicle that was objectively uncomfortable to the world, but subjectively comfortable to James. The hum of the AM radio was the only noise that ever came out of those speakers. He wasn't convinced the radio had an FM dial – even though the faceplate said so. The station often played songs about working people and jobs. The songs were a comfort to James. If he was ever out and about and heard one of the songs (a rarity), he would be instantly transported back to

1979. If labor had a smell, it was in that truck, and he would instantly smell it. No matter the temperature, he would instantly feel somewhat warm. He would feel as safe as he ever had.

Joe Hill's "Rebel Girl" softly drifted throughout the car. Joe began to sing along; he had heard the song enough times that he mindlessly voiced the lyrics – not completely knowing what they meant. In the middle of the song, James asked his dad about the rebel girl, or as he said it, the Confederate girl. His dad pulled the truck over and looked at him. The look his father gave him was piercing and it worried him that he was about to be told something that would be so life-altering that he would always divide his life into two eras: before that truck ride and after it.

He went on to explain the song and was serious in saying "The Rebel Girl is a working-class hero, not a traitor." His father took this very seriously and it confused Joe – he had never seen his father care about something that seemed so trivial. The memory or the knowledge never left him. He would always think of that conversation whenever he heard the song – he would hear the song a lot in his life, and he would think about that moment every time. He never thought about it as a good or bad memory, just an influential one. Over time, he would grow to appreciate the time his dad took to share with him something that seemingly meant that much to him.

All The Things That Could Be

This story came into view as he parked his car across from the picket line in front of an assembly factory. There must have been hundreds of people lining the roads, thrusting signs into the air and pulling them back down to the earth as if they were afraid that if left up long enough, they would have been snatched into heaven. The striking workers made him think about both of his parents, both of whom engaged in them. They were very honest and transparent with James about what they were doing and why they were doing it.

He was extremely interested in what was happening on the other side of the road, not that unions were foreign to him (he had been in one in his brief stint in education) but he never saw labor truly organized in the way that was demonstrated in front of him. It looked powerful. But that could have been nothing in comparison to what it should have been. Maybe this was such a small section of the workforce who were demanding outrageously unrealistic conditions, ones that James would have been ashamed to be in awe of.

"Let's go check this out." He was in his age of information. He had traveled quite a distance to get out to the Midwest and he had a lot of time to think about things in his life and gather information along the way. He had learned to ask better questions and what to do with the information he had gathered. The shame of not knowing was now leaving his system. If he wanted to know about something, it was time to simply ask. How easy was that?

He walked across to the double yellow lines before putting it into a small trot to guarantee his safe passage. He came up to a group of strikers who all wore faces that looked cautious of the stranger's arrival. They had experienced all the emotions, words, and actions of passerbyers since the strike began, and their suspicion was warranted.

"Hi. Can we help you?" a shorter woman with a demeanor and appearance of absolutism spoke for the group. No one protested her taking the lead, they seemed to expect it.

"Yeah, I was just curious what was going on here. What are you guys striking for?" James laid out exactly the information he wanted before them. The absolute woman looked perplexed like she was being pranked. "Excuse me?"

"I see you are UAW" he pointed to the sign, "and I know you are striking" he gestured to the crowd, "I want to know what's going on."

"Are you press?"

"Nah. But my father was a big-time union guy, it's something I grew up on and have an interest in."

She looked around the group with uncertainty. This stranger was not on the list of people they anticipated showing up. The other strikers shrugged and put the decision back on the leader. They wanted to share their message, their cause – but they all wanted to know who they were telling what, even though in the end they are most likely telling everyone the same thing. There was a sense of control retained by making it seem like only selective people got the information they wanted. Control was something these workers didn't feel they had, so they felt the need to guard it when they had it.

Molly, the head of the picket squad, gave James a brief rundown about what they were up against. The demands were very similar to other factories in all cities across the country. Pay too low, lack of job protection, days off – the works. These were the common normal striking pieces, often very achievable if not for the Smaug-like owners and management who may or may not have been bathing in profits – literally and figuratively. James didn't understand, he was aware of this kind of thing, as most middle-class workers were, but figured that some chemical was released in your head when you got to a certain level in a corporation, or at a certain salary. It was something that he and his ilk simply would not be able to comprehend – they were just not motivated enough to comprehend life like that.

The rest of the workers continued to shout, march, preach, and believe up and down the line. Molly spread the cause. The more she talked with James, the more she sensed his desire to truly be informed of their plight. There was no malice in his wondering.

"If you want to know more, meet down at Bill's Tavern on Madison. We have a meeting once a week to talk it over. 7 PM."

All The Things That Could Be

James nodded and thanked Molly for her time. He wished the crowd good luck for the rest of the day and turned around to head back across the street. As he turned and faced the street, a cherry red car ripped by at speeds not meant for that road. A hand came out the window expressing their dissatisfaction with the striking workers accompanied with the slogan, "Go back to work, you bums!" From the back seat, a projectile was launched, and James took it straight in the chest. When it hit him, it exploded. In every direction flew bits of sandwich. Peanut butter and jelly – James could tell right away.

"Get that license plate!" Yelled Molly. A cacophony of angry voices rang out in unison as they showed their disgust at the drive-by. The car was gone before Molly could finish her sentence.

"It's blacked out! It's blacked out!" Someone came with a purpose.

"Jesus, are you okay?" Molly came up and comforted him – he was not injured but he was a little shaken up by it. He wasn't even picketing, just at the wrong place at the wrong time, he reasoned. What impact did these workers, who wanted better for their families and the friends of their coworkers, have on them? Were quality living conditions a zero-sum game? Only a certain number of people could have it, and when they did it was at the expense of others. The hatred that poured out of that vehicle was astounding to

James. Sure, he had heard about it, read about it, and known about it – but today he was victimized by it.

"Yeah, I am. Thanks." He brushed down on his flannel multiple times clearing everything off the best he could. He got it though. Right in the chest. He then laughed. "I'll see you at 7."

The other workers had gathered around to see the pantry assassination attempt. They marveled at how well he took the hit. Bits of sandwich were everywhere. A worker in the crowd who had paid attention to the conversation from afar between Molly and James could tell that he was a comrade through Molly's body language. From the densely packed group, he yelled, "All hail the Sandwich Man! Friend of the struggle!"

"Sandwich Man!" erupted the other voices ebulliently.

A trip to the launder and the local YMCA was calling his name. After that, it was time to find a library to brush up on his history.

17

He was the absolute worst and she hated him more than anyone she had hated in her life. She hated him most because nobody saw it, and nobody believed her. He was the epitome of charisma to others, but to her, he was a snake, a predator.

Molly Flynn had worked on the factory floor for fifteen years. For the last seven years, she had to put up with the floor supervisor harassing her in the shadows and threatening her with the terms of her employment. Why she had become his sole victim was completely unknown to her. She had complained to human resources and was all but laughed out of the office. There was no punishment for this man – he was invincible. He had berated her, touched her, and humiliated her – sometimes all at once, sometimes the punishments took turns.

An only child from Jacksonville, Florida – she was diminutive in size and stature. She had long, flat, amber hair that flowed like waterfalls over the sides of her head. She embraced her poor vision with wireframe glasses. A few freckles marked her fair cheeks and she burned easier than she tanned. For as unassuming as she looked, she commanded the presence of those around her. She was impressive.

For so long she was so timid. She felt lucky just to have the job she had moved to the Midwest for. She knew it was a good-paying job, a relatively stable job, and it came with benefits. She had foregone a shot at a college education (she thinks, never actually applied anywhere) to start making money right away. She had been turned off by the idea of college – in part because she had no idea what she wanted to do. Molly looked at this opportunity to give her some guidance on whether that decision was a good one or if she should have trundled through two years in the hopes of finding something she loved or was good at and then declare two more years in pursuit of it.

From the beginning of her senior year, she looked for future opportunities, emailing prospective employers and sometimes receiving a message back, often some canned and insincere message. She found it patronizing, especially since she was a year away from being part of the labor force they would seek. The only person who sent back a message that she felt satisfied with was a floor supervisor at the job she was currently at. Molly applied there and got the job.

However, the floor supervisor who hired her eventually was promoted and moved to another position in another building, and then they hired a person who would soon make Molly's work life a living hell. Not immediately, but eventually. She kept her ear to the street for hiring opportunities, but nothing had managed to pull her from her current position. She felt like she had been blacklisted, by who she could only guess.

All The Things That Could Be

Molly had built up a couple of years in the company and thought she could maneuver her way out of the new supervisor's predatory line of sight or get transferred somewhere else. A recession later and more NAFTA promises kept the workers tranquil – happy to just hold on to what they had. There had been talk about striking for a couple of years, but nothing materialized – even as the recession accordioned back, the threat of their factory moving to a place where the uppity-ups could take advantage of workers (also read as make profits from not paying workers) as a rate only dreamed of.

"If you ever say anything, I promise you'll never get another job as long as I breathe." A haunting statement which she could still feel the heat of his breath on her as he threatened. It was a sentence that unnerved her, a barrier that she had a tough time seeing over. There were small breaks in time where it didn't impact her and there were others where it caused cortisol to pump into her veins on hyperdrive. She wanted nothing more than to be free of the prison she was put in, but her fears were paramount.

She was respected by her fellow workers – seen as a beacon of trust and reliability. She often helped others when she had the opportunity and taught others the best ways to accomplish their tasks. Molly was all about quality control. She had done or dabbled in most of the other jobs, so she understood the ins, outs, and oddities of them all. She knew what worked, but most importantly, she knew what didn't work. She could spot a problem simply from the technique that someone used. She was quick to correct, and her team valued her for that. The team made for a very efficient floor.

Her team had no idea about the harassment. They had no idea about Heath.

Heath floated like a ghost between areas to ensure that everything was on the up and up and deadlines were being hit. He was a bit of a mystery and a quiet guy. Molly's team knew a few things: he was loved by management, and he was quite unknown outside of work. If you ever asked anything about him, people seemed to get amnesia, or they never knew to begin with. Neither of these facts they loved, but they also knew the political side of business and as far as that went, he was a sure thing to stay at that company. It was because of these two facts that Molly never said anything. The reward did not outweigh the risk.

The harassment always happened when she could prove it the least. The pattern was set by an enigma, a code that she could not crack or recognize. Situations that differed from day to day – she had been harassed or touched in one scenario but play that scenario out again one hundred more times and it wouldn't happen. But it might be on the one hundred and first. Molly sometimes wondered if there were two, three, or four Heaths that worked in the factory, they just took turns occupying the same body. She never allowed it to be used as a free pass though.

Once, she had told someone (outside of human resources) and got laughed at. She kept the secret from there on out. Molly recognized that it wasn't the healthiest thing to do, but she also wasn't sure how to handle it. If the people who were hired to believe her, didn't believe her, who would? She also used this information to plot. She would eventually get her revenge, but she didn't know how. She had tried a couple of times to record conversations and even once strapped her phone to her body and cut out a tiny hole for the camera's eye – none of it worked. The strap left a rash.

She attempted to avoid him the best she could, but he seemed to be everywhere when no one else was around. She was prideful and refused to show weakness, but sometimes her pride walked her into situations where she would be victimized. Moving past where parts were inventoried, Heath's hand would find part of her body, a word here, a comment there. She knew she would eventually have her day in the sun, and since the powers that be found such a prize in Heath, she knew it might be up to the vigilante side to see justice administered.

As a woman in the field, she was now in her thirties and had a presence in the factory that commanded respect from many. She was often lauded for her abilities and methods of teaching. For as much praise and accolades as she received, she was never offered promotions outside of the factory, only inside it. She had an idea why.

Unbeknownst to her, her issues were made significantly worse when Heath walked around the corner into an unsuspecting gathering of workers and heard one say,

All The Things That Could Be

"Man, they gotta get Molly to be the floor supe. She's way more qualified than anyone who has been here since I have." Heath took that information and locked it away.

The straw that broke the camel's back was when Heath went after a couple of Molly's workers. One day, men in blue business suits came down to talk with Heath (maybe it was a flex of power, Molly never knew why they couldn't have done it in an email or private conversation), after some small talk deliberation, Heath pointed to two men who were busily working away and talking amongst themselves, if they could be heard through the masks and the noise. Heath was well aware that Molly was tuned into the conversation and turned to her and winked as the men in the blue-pressed suits left.

Not good, Molly thought.

The next day, word had got around that a round of unexpected layoffs had come about and those two were selected as expendable. They were getting the axe. One of them just had his second child and the other was consistently working overtime to ensure he could put his kid through medical school.

Layoffs? Molly was aware of how the company was rolling along and layoffs were about the furthest thing from necessary that there was – as far as need went. The company was making money hand over fist, they didn't need layoffs.

All The Things That Could Be

Molly sleuthed around from different parts of the factory and talked to people in similar roles. They had seen the stories in the paper about the CEO bonus and the payout from the sex scandal still fresh from the head of human resources (of course it was human resources). If the company was hemorrhaging money, it was because it couldn't stop beating its skull with a hammer.

"What do the heads at UAW think about this?" Molly's suggested statement was in the form of a question.

"Haven't heard too much. It's still fresh. I think they are looking into it." A couple of floor workers had gathered around, they admired Molly.

"What does local leadership think?" Molly smirked.

"I don't know, Molly, what do you think?" A few of the guys in the circle laughed, she knew what she was doing.

"You know what I think. Gather some more information. If this is as bad as it smells, I think is it time to pull the trigger on a walkout."

"Lots of risk there."

"Yeah. I'll talk to some of the others and let's see if this is a realistic win for us. The company doesn't look good with some of the new headlines, we could strike while the iron is hot."

"Anything better with Heath?"

All The Things That Could Be

"No."

18

James buzzed over to the YMCA for a quick swim and lift and also to clean up from the drive-by sandwiching. He kept finding crumbs and stains here and there, but he now had a story to tell. The journey so far had yielded a few stories, certainly.

After he cleaned up, he kept checking his watch to make sure he had not impeded on the time that he had promised to meet the local union. The time wasn't even close, but he checked it religiously.

The information that Molly gave up freely impressed him and saddened him. He knew the immense risk it took to stand on that line, he ended up wearing some of it. He wondered about the times his father or mother would have been on the line, did they ever get sandwiched? What did they have yelled at them? What did people *do* to them? These are thoughts he never ruminated on, but now that he did, he began to feel flush in the face. A quiet heat crept up his neck and into his face.

Those who felt empowered to do such knew that they were just nameless, faceless rabble that would never be held accountable for the things they said or did. The ignorance was more stunning than the harassment – how much could you know about the struggle just from driving by and looking at some signs? He began to feel upset. But he knew that occasionally he made irrational decisions based on in-the-moment feelings and those feelings typically resided. The post-anger clarity was always refreshing, he was especially glad when he didn't overreact in a situation. James attempted to never act out of feeling.

The incident did pique his interest and of all the free things he thought about during his planning two of them always popped out to him: the YMCA and libraries. Libraries were the last bastion of peace and welcoming. Everyone could come to the library and read their books, and magazines, use their computers, and listen to their music. Libraries were clean and quiet, and the people who worked at them were very kind. They were the closest thing to a utopia that you find nowadays. They ask for nothing, except for you to check back from time to time.

Upon stepping into the library, he immediately asked for assistance. "Labor history?" An instant answer pointed him in the right direction. No guessing, no games, no fees, no ads – just answering. The library.

James wasn't totally ignorant of labor history; he had read some more modern works – enough to know that there was a group of people who benefited because they used a larger group of people to make them money. He knew of the way groups were exploited, he knew of Pinkertons and some of the ways people resisted. He wanted to dig into it more. He wanted to learn more about the specific struggles that blue-collar workers suffered through to make changes for the betterment of everybody.

All The Things That Could Be

A couple of books on the shelves caught his eye, ones that he felt were forbidden reads. Books that made him feel like he was doing something wrong, even though he wasn't. Namely among those were the works of Marx. Reading with or agreeing with Marx was something he felt might still earn you a blacklisting. He pulled the book down quickly to his side and made sure that his arm covered the entire cover and spine. He then felt ashamed of his feeling ashamed. It was silly, but it was.

Then, he plopped down at a table and began to read voraciously. He could read quickly and comprehend deeply – a skill he always had. He was able to power through texts, even those as complex as *Das Kapital* with clarity and speed. He moved through the text and made notes on a notepad he had purchased on the road. Themes, quotes, ideas – the entirety of it made sense to him. He understood the views of Marx and understood why his country was so against him learning about it. He always knew *about* his work, but now he was digging into such forbidden fruit.

After he put down such radical learnings, James looked through microfilms and other periodicals about strikes and movements that had taken place in the United States. In newspaper clippings, he found pictures of men who looked like him and women who looked like Molly. Men who looked like his father, and women who looked like his mother. People who smiled and people who frowned. People who celebrated good and who mourned bad. They were an amalgamation of all workers, staring back at him in those

All The Things That Could Be

fragile sepia photos. He realized at that moment that while he never knew anyone who had been fighting on the side of workers, he had probably known hundreds.

The library was ready to close, which meant it was time for his next meeting of the day – Bill's Tavern on Madison. He had printed off a map while at the library to help him find this location of middle-class strife and made his way. The sun slowly began to dip beyond the horizon: a swirl of colors dazzled the skies, looking at it too long could cause an accident.

The drive from the library was not too long, he navigated up and down different side streets and got to witness families preparing themselves for the last few hours of the day. Yards were populated with kids, moms, and dads as they played various games or did various chores. Appreciating the sight, one that he remembered being a part of as a kid, he drove contently to Bill's. As he rolled toward the old neon sign, he saw a dingy building with nearly all the street parking spots around it filled up. He had got there just a tad early, so he was witnessing many of those from the picket lines entering in – after they warmly greeted one another.

Opening the door, a dull hum of noise came from within, a soft warm glow met his eyes and he saw Molly right away in the back corner. He felt quite serendipitous for finding her so immediately, considering how small she was. He made his way by tables and peanut shells that littered the floor. Large glasses of beer were found on any tables where people could be found.

The owner of the bar was a large and imposing man. All his hair had migrated from his head to his face some years ago, it seemed as if he didn't ever pay attention to it beyond that. He wore a remarkably clean waist apron and a button-up white shirt. It was tough to see how bright the shirt was in the dingy light. His arms erupted through his rolled-up sleeves, if there was ever a bartender built to throw some drunk through a window, he was the guy.

Three billiards tables attracted a crowd at the back of the tavern opposite Molly. Balls clacked and clattered over the soft music and voices that penetrated the air. As he approached, Molly turned toward him and threw her hands out in surprise. "Wow, I honestly did not think you would make it here. I see the sandwich didn't keep you down too long."

"Not too long. I am a tough guy like that." He joked right back.

One of the workers from the line noticed him, and James wasn't sure if he was three sheets to the wind or just incredibly friendly, but he yelled, "Sandwich Man!" and a few cheers broke from the crowd. Molly grinned and said, "Some of the guys were worried about you taking the hit. They are happy you made it out alive." Someone handed James a beer, and he nodded. Molly then signaled with her eyes in the direction of the bar where more people were starting to filter.

All The Things That Could Be

James entered the area of the gathering but felt as if he lacked the clout and seniority (which he had zero) to claim a chair, so he casually hung out against the wall. Molly had already pulled up a chair, as it screeched across the floor. She then abandoned it midway to go and stand with James. She recognized something in him that was pure and true. If he was some modern-day Pinkerton or some company spy, his aura was deceptive. She felt she typically had a pretty good bead on people.

As more and more filtered in, so came the bartender. Even amongst the low murmur that was occurring as they waited for the speaker to bring the meeting to order, the barkeep put both hands on his hips, breathed in, and then projected loudly to everyone in the room, "You give 'em hell today?" The workers roared with delight.

"You know it!"

"Another day!"

"We will break 'em soon!"

Confidence from the excitement soon filled up the room and it proved to be the perfect segue for the speaker.

"Alright, alright, alright." A big-bearded man stood upon a lectern and immediately captured the attention of the entire group. He was wearing a shirt that barely fit, his arms rippled as he grabbed the sides of the podium. He had markings on his face that looked like grease, but James couldn't tell.

All The Things That Could Be

"Nothing much new with negotiations, but there is something they aren't telling us yet. I am not sure if it has to do with negative press adding up or what, but I feel like if we keep the clamps on, we will see victory soon enough." A disappointed sigh went through the room.

A smattering of conversation slithered around the tables, the talk of bills, food, family, money, rent, insurance, caretaking, school, daycare – all very real problems that cost very real dollars. The strike funds would be depleted eventually – and everyone would have to cut back on the enjoyable things in life to ensure everyone could survive.

The speaker recognized the doubts and the tinge of regret some workers had in their voices. With as much as he could muster, he crushed the dissent with a powerful reminder, "We knew this would be tough. We know they have more money and more resources to outlast us. We must hold together! Do not let the small discomforts ruin how much you have already done! Suffer today for a better tomorrow. If not for you, then for any worker who comes after you, including your children." It was as if he had a magic wand that snapped people out of their spell of nonbelief. They looked down at the ground as if they were ashamed for questioning the cause. The near nonbelievers then raised their heads, some clapped and a few slapped the table. Born anew.

An impressionable man, James was captivated by the speaker. He went on to speak of the injustices that the

All The Things That Could Be

company tried to normalize in the workplace – things Molly had spoken of.

He turned toward Molly and asked, "What can I do?"

"What do you mean, you're not even part of this? What do you care?" She blasted back. She couldn't make heads or tails of James, only recognizing his good intentions. "Don't you have your own job?" She remained flabbergasted.

James gave her a rundown on himself, what she needed to know to make sense of him at that moment, and a little bit sprinkled in of extra. He referred to the robbery in Montana and how he nearly destroyed some loose livestock heading through Kansas.

Molly's face was consumed with a quizzical look and right then she felt as if her radar had lied to her, she couldn't believe James' story to be real. What a bizarre story. It would only be made more bizarre if it were made up to try and impress someone, however.

The speaker scanned the crowd, and James followed his eyes. Once his eyes reached the place where Molly was planning to sit, they jumped wildly across the room when he couldn't find her. Then, their eyes locked for a brief second when Molly was located. He stepped down from his position and strolled confidently through the crowd toward the small leader. She recognized the hulking man and turned toward him; she opened a position for him in the conversation and he stepped in – towering over them both.

"Roland, this is James. James. Roland."

James stuck out his hand and for a split second wondered if it was a good idea. He saw Roland's hand come toward his like a python, it was going to squeeze, and it was going to hurt. The anticipation was for not, the leader recognized the concern and worry (he was well versed) and was gentle.

"Welcome. Thanks for coming." His voice seemed deeper up close. Barely visible tattoos marked the arms and neck of his dark skin. A short haircut and a long silver chain adorned his head and neck.

"James wants to help."

"Which building are you in?" Roland forward faced James to ask him this.

"Uh. None." James gave back an answer that confused Roland. Molly chimed in to complete the story. "He doesn't work for Potrix."

"He doesn't work with us?"

"Nope."

Roland squinted at Molly then at James, and then back to Molly. His eyes then beamed into Molly the question, "What is going on here?"

James intervened to spare Molly from having to tell the somewhat unbelievable story.

The massive unit of a man followed the tale with a skepticism which he told in his body language, visible to anyone within a couple of miles. James noticed it but took no offense. He sometimes couldn't believe what he was doing himself.

"So let me sum this up. You are just…driving…no real destination. Your folks were long-time union members, and so this is your version of luck finding us. And now you want to help? What did I miss?"

Nodding along with each word, Roland didn't miss much. It was impossible to believe if you weren't living it, the way James was. He had broken away from the chains of wage labor, something even Cesar Chavez, Bill Haywood, and Eugene Debs would only have dreamed of. Mind you, his breaking away from the chains didn't come with a contingency plan, something the aforementioned would have needed to execute such a scheme.

"You want to join the line? Come on out. There is always a sign to be waved." Roland shrugged.

"If that is what you need, I can do it. I am happy to do more if needed." James was disappointed by the mundane suggestion, but he also couldn't have been asked to step up to the bargaining table. He thought maybe somewhere in between would have best suited him, but not even he knew what role that might encompass. Maybe they would ask him to sabotage a plant or something. What he did know was he had time and no official ties to the union itself. He was a bit of a wildcard in this regard.

"I am not associated with your union. I know how they work outside of the boundaries to union bust. Maybe if we pretended that we never met at this meeting – no one might associate us together – and then I can help in a different way." James could hardly believe the nonsense that was spewing out of his mouth. What was he even saying? Was he offering to blow up a plant or kidnap some CEO's dog? It was a bit foolish.

Roland and Molly looked at one another and back at James. They, too, tried to decode what he was suggesting. The interest was there, but the details were murky.

"James. This is the wildest conversation I think I have ever had in this role. Just…keep showing up. We will have something for you to do." Roland spit the words out and Molly laughed.

19

Days turned into a couple of weeks and James continued to mingle with the workers, out holding signs like Roland suggested. His desire to become more involved was increasing at a dramatic pace. James felt underutilized and thought he could be a bigger piece of the movement if only given a chance. While he marched on the line and better learned of the struggle afterward, he felt he was developing a camaraderie amongst the workers. They had accepted him and welcomed him warmly to the line every morning. He never took from the strike fund or even considered it, but he would accept coffee and sandwiches made from those funds for those on the line.

Roland continued his message which was the equivalent of "the war will be over by Christmas" and the spirit for the strike would wax and wane. James had not been a victim of another drive-by sandwiching – just the occasional expletive. There seemed to be more cheers than boos, however.

The press had started to cover the story a little more. Reports for the newspaper would come out and even the local nightly news would set the camera up on the tripod and roll some footage for a few moments, now and again bringing in one of the workers on the line. Molly had her face on camera and her words in the newspaper a few times.

All The Things That Could Be

Neither side continued to budge and there were rumors of scab workers being used to replace those who were currently not there. Roland, Molly, and other leadership began to talk openly about the next steps. James marched every hour of the day, he believed Roland and Molly put him there for maximum effectiveness, but with each passing hour and the needle hardly moving, he spent his time marching and scheming.

Back in the cozy confines of the library early in the morning, James continued to research information regarding this new, or at least potential, opportunity. He continued to read through labor history, great speeches of history, the local plant itself, and most interesting, the scandal that had rocked the plant time and time again. From sex scandals to money laundering, the company was often in the news for one nefarious reason or another. He came across many articles and was able to read plenty about it. He read about the company getting bailed out during the recession – they begged the government to give them a hefty payday or they would need to cut the workforce. They got the money they wanted, but they still cut the workforce.

He dug deeper.

A few years later, the company was engaged in stock buybacks.

James wondered how many people were let go and told, "Well, you should have saved money for reasons like this. You can't expect someone else to help you out. You need to be responsible and prepare for the unexpected." He was saddened and upset by the thought.

All this damning evidence of corporate malfeasance and they were putting their boot on the workers' necks? He didn't like it, but he had an idea. He gathered as many headlines as he could about the company and started photocopying the headlines and bylines. He was able to find fifteen different pieces, each one more damning than the next. He started taking the headlines and combining them onto a single paper – a poster of lies and deception. A poster of ill deeds, a poster of money being wasted because of foolishness and greed. James wondered if the court of public opinion could pressure the company into negotiating.

He worked clandestinely – the fewer people who had eyes on his doings, the better. The more plausible deniability he had, the better. As he worked diligently, cutting, taping, searching, angling – shut out everything around him. He was working with a single-track mind. Laser focus.

"Well, well – working hard, I see." A familiar voice whispered through the library and broke his concentration. He covered his work and turned around to Molly, standing with her arms crossed and a smile on her face. "What do you have here?" She began to rifle through some of the cutout materials and read each one carefully.

"Wow, you have been busy here. What are you planning to do with this?" Molly inquired while continuing to read each headline and byline.

All The Things That Could Be

James found the reason not worth lying about, so he was honest with the woman, he felt like she already knew the answer to the question anyway. "Well, I thought if I composed all this together and spread it out around the area, maybe it would turn support away from the plant and to you guys." Her smile left.

"Ah, your heart is in the right place. I appreciate it. But we can't do this." He gestured widely to the poster. "If this gets out, they will think it is us. They will assume we are trying to embarrass them, and it won't play." It was a realistic backfire which James did not calculate in his holy fervor.

She placed a soft hand on his shoulder as she could feel the excitement leaving him. "It is pretty badass – I wouldn't mind keeping this one for myself." He slid the paper over to her and began gathering up the scraps of paper. James had to believe that she was right, he felt embarrassed for not considering it. He could have torpedoed the entire strike with his good intentions – at least he was stopped. However, he had learned a lot about a lot. He was not sorry for the information he had gathered over the last couple of weeks.

"What is the word on negotiations?" James asked. He hadn't heard any news for a while and was interested in learning, but not very hopeful about the answer he believed he would get.

"Roland thinks they are bringing in scabs to put the pressure on us."

All The Things That Could Be

"What are you going to do?" He recognized that the real threat of replacement workers would very much undermine the cause and put the workers in a lose-lose scenario. The threat of replacement workers would cause others to cross the picket line and go back to work. Some already had.

James had read about a lot of conventional ways and unconventional ways. He listed them off, many of them Molly was familiar with.

Sick outs? Slowdowns? Sit downs? All possibilities.

The first two carried enough plausible deniability. The last one was certainly the most effective in a complete shutdown of work. A combination of these may be effective. James was hesitant to suggest them because he knew he would no longer be able to take part. He wanted to remain useful. He would do what he could to continue to be of use. He reminded himself that this was not about him, he was merely there to assist where he could.

***

As another night at Bill's came around, the discussion had changed. Whether it was his conversation with Molly or the general understanding that the tactics employed were not effective enough to be still considered.

All The Things That Could Be

The crowd at Bill's had thinned — James feared the strike was losing momentum and the workers would ultimately be forced back into their positions with nothing to show for and a puffed-up management who would remember it until the day each one of them was fired before they could collect a pension.

Roland laid out the plan — a slowdown. He said there was enough deniability that it would be tough to pinpoint anyone directly, but he did warn that it didn't mean it was consequence-free. Anyone of them at any time could be let go — it came with the territory. The slowdown also meant no replacement workers — they would give the company a little bit of what they wanted, it may have seemed like a concession, but ultimately it was sabotage.

As the message was first delivered it seemed to fall upon deaf ears and stone-cold faces. These people had been in the trenches for weeks on end, with little relief in the immediate future. Some of them only came to the meetings because it was the route their car had known at that time on that day of the week. Roland pressed on, his voice raised, and his hands cut through the air wildly. He was fired up and trying to transfer his energy to the crowd. As the plan was laid out specifically in more detail, stone-cold, war-torn vets turned into true believers. James saw them start to turn, and so did Roland. Once he noticed it, he let loose and gave it all he had. He poured on the labor message and the crowd began to eat it up. They were satiated soon after Roland began. He urged his members not to give it, and to continue bolstering the cause for others. Victory came through holding firm.

James felt himself leaving the effort. He was not sure what more he could do. Picketing outside was one thing, but he could not put himself into the factory and continue to pretend to be an employee.

"Molly, I think my time is done here. I have done what I could to help and thank you for the opportunity." Molly felt sadness and she felt that James' selflessness in helping their strike get somewhere gave him purpose – something that she felt he was searching for. They had both helped one another.

James shook hands with the other workers in the tavern and they addressed him by his moniker – Sandwich Man. Hugs were given, and thoughtful messages were exchanged.

Molly and Roland walked James outside and they had an extended goodbye. "Your pops would be proud of the support you've given us. We won't quit, and we won't forget." Roland gripped his hand, Molly hugged him.

James drove away to a rest area on the other side of town where he parked for the night. He settled in between two semis – he had found assurance in being hugged by two big rigs. His car was obfuscated by the massive shadows cast by the trucks – nearly invisible to anyone who wasn't specifically looking for it.

All The Things That Could Be

As he was able to crawl into the back of the car and get rest for the night, he noticed something familiar – which was particularly odd because he was so far away from home, and nothing here should be too familiar. A beautiful, cherry-red car slowly motored past his car, illuminated by the semi's light. He immediately put the foreign object in a different setting and, like two puzzle pieces lining up, a sense of accomplishment washed over him. He looked at the license plate, and while James was not a vengeful human, a feeling of fear came across him.

A blacked-out license place.

The feeling of coincidence was not with him at that moment, why this car was pulling up near the dead of night in this area was curious. He felt it was out of place.

Two figures stepped out of the car and began moving in the direction of James' car. For a second, he felt like the hunter, but with every step, he began to feel hunted. Closer and closer they came, James tried to stay as still as he could – a nice little trick he learned from Jurassic Park. But they were not deterred by movie magic moves, each of them split the car and ended up on each side.

The hard knocking of knuckles on glass reverberated in James' car. Since he was in the backseat, he didn't know if they knew he was there. Then he considered the consequences if they didn't believe he was in the car – so he opened the door.

"Can I help you, gentlemen?" He played it off as if he had never seen the car before and thought the politeness would be understood as ignorance – and that the men could then go on their way. No harm, no foul. Just keep it moving.

"Step out of the car." A voice with zero variation and a quite serious inflection. A needle moved in James' mind. How much danger he was may have been rising. He knew who they probably were, the car and license plate were a giveaway to him, but he couldn't be sure that they knew what he knew. So, he continued to play aloof.

"I'm sorry, am I not allowed to camp overnight here?"

"Please, step out of the car." Both men tried to open the doors. Two plans jumped into James' mind. He could make a break for the front seat, start the car, and drive away. This would take a significant amount of time and he was unsure the of business these men meant and to what means they would be willing to go to accomplish said business. The other was to take his chances of playing the aloof fool.

"I think there has been some sort of mix-up here, gentlemen. I am just traveling through." James stepped out of the car and one of the men grabbed him by the arm and escorted him away.

"Where are you taking me?" The question was met with silence.

Then, "Make any attempts at anything foolish, and it will be a really bad move."

They walked back to the car, located in the shadows, and pushed him in. In the back was a man who was smoking a cigarette. The red glow pulsated into the low light, his face was only visible during puffs, and even then, he couldn't have picked him out in a lineup.

"Who are you?" the man exhaled a plume of smoke and asked the question almost simultaneously – James thought he must have done this before.

"James." His ID was in the car, he figured that lying and being found out could cause more problems than just owning up.

"Who do you work for?" The man demanded an answer that he wouldn't believe. James raced in his mind to come up with a solution to this problem. He imagined the men were strikebreakers of some sort – modern-day Pinkterons, maybe even cops doing a side hustle. Or maybe a main hustle.

"I don't work for anybody. I told your friends here, I am just traveling through." A truth that he knew would not be believed.

"Then what is this." He held up the composite of newspaper articles and bylines made about the company. James had only made one of those and Molly had taken it. More questions ran through his head. Was Molly safe? Was

Molly a traitor? Who was Molly? Did she set him up? Was she alive? Did she get a visit? Each question seemed to have a low percentage answer, but when the pie was divided up ten ways, the winning choice still only had a ten percent chance of being picked.

"Some newspaper clipping. Big deal. All public knowledge." James decided to try and take a different stance, something more combative, making himself seem like a threat. If he could create some fuzziness and confusion around him, and what he did or who he knew, perhaps he would get out of this unscathed.

"Who do you work for?" The same question in the same tone.

"Very powerful people, who go to very far extremes to accomplish their goals." It was perhaps the biggest lie that James had ever told. But he felt like he passed with his acting. He sounded stern and a bit menacing. He sounded like he had protection around him constantly, but they too hid in the shadows.

The cigarette man received a reply he did not anticipate and did not have a response loaded up. So, there he sat, thinking about what to say. He did not know if James was lying or not, and errored on the side of believing that too irrational of action could yield unpleasant results. Could there be a "him counterpart" out there? Could there be a new striking labor protection strategy or agency that employs the same thuggish intimidation that the biggest corporations did?

All The Things That Could Be

This was new information. Threatening enough to not hurt or take this mysterious man. But they would be watching, he informed James.

"No more. Our next meeting with have consequences."

Silence felt like the best answer to the question. It didn't provoke, but it also didn't show fear. It was an answer that had a wide range of interpretations, he could choose whichever suited him. Either way, James was getting released from this insane situation.

He got back into his car, the hum of the diesel engines that surrounded him droned on as he thought, and then said aloud, "What the hell was that?"

This situation quickly went from normal to nuts. He was now being targeted by some company thugs for a half-cooked idea. He was living out of his car, sleeping in whatever town he parked in. This was the stuff of movies or comic books, not real life. He felt like his journey was getting out of control, and for a few moments, he closed his eyes and pretended he was back home. In his mind, to prove he wasn't greedy, in the event of deity or djinn was present, he imagined himself at work, rather than warm in his bed.

***

All The Things That Could Be

James woke up to fog rolling over the empty parking lot. He had to take a moment to decipher the events before. He thought about Molly and immediately drove over to the plant, the strikers were marching and waiting. He parked in the same spot he always did and went across the way where he saw the squad of picketers he knew best. "Sandwich Man!" one yelled. Hoots and hollers immediately followed.

At this point, James assumed he was being watched. He quickly found Molly.

"I got a visit last night."

Molly looked at him and laughed. He sounded like he was in a movie. "A visit from who?"

James told the story about the men coming up to his car, escorting him away and how they put him in the car, showed him the collage he had made (that she took), the threat, and the conversation.

Molly looked frozen with fear or confusion, he wasn't sure which, but it didn't look great. James was afraid that he knew the answer to why. "They broke into your place, didn't they?"

Stunned silence and a quick nod. "When I got home last night, my deadbolt wasn't locked, just my bottom lock. I *always* lock both of them. Always. I cannot emphasize or underscore that enough. This is not good. We must act."

James was not sure what "act" meant in this context, but it sounded like some sort of contingency plan was already in place.

"Act? How? Also – remember the car that sandwiched me? I think it was the same car there last night." James spewed the words out.

"What? Really?" Molly didn't know what to do with the new information. On the one hand, it made some sense: perhaps they were trying strike-breaking methods at different levels. Low levels get sandwich throwings and high levels get threatening the lives of members. Seemed fair.

"Damn, they assume since you don't work at the company that you must be from another group. They feel like this adds to our resolve to not cross. So, they are upping their methods to ensure that we do." A stream of consciousness played out in front of James as Molly looked at the ground and connected the dots in her head.

"How do they know that I don't work here?"

The people who could have been behind this just considerably narrowed. Someone inside the company must have recognized this new striker as someone who wasn't also involved on the floor. Furthermore, thousands were on strike, it would have been difficult for some overseer to know everyone on the line and be able to identify somebody new.

The call seemed to be coming from inside the house.

All The Things That Could Be

There was no shortage of people who wanted the strike to end, and by end, they meant workers got nothing, so profits were not cut into. But the number of people who might have figured out that James wasn't one of the tens of thousands of nameless faces all working towards a single goal was smaller, but still large enough that they would be in it for the long haul.

Lots of employees also meant many people in management. Whoever it was would not be easy to find, and they had to come to terms that they may never find out. That was a bit of a frightening thought, if the company was greenlighting violence to protect the bottom line, how far would they go to do it?

He felt like he was deeper on the messy side of strikes than he had ever heard about – and that includes the one his father fought in. He was being deliberately targeted by powerful people and it was only his anonymity and his bluffing that possibly kept him afloat. A knot turned in his stomach because Molly didn't have the answer that he thought she should. He most hoped for her to say something like "First time getting visited?" as if it were something that just happened to the people involved. He knew better, but he hoped all the same.

"Molly, this is a little too much. I mean, I want to help but I feel like I have crossed over into a whole other realm with this. I expected resistance but I didn't expect to die for this." He nervously stammered his way through the sentence. As the sentence fell out of his mouth he started to understand. People weren't given their rights, they weren't given better conditions, better pay, more safety, and everything in between. They had to fight for it, and sometimes people died for it.

Quitting now would be giving in.

20

The strike moved along slowly. James felt like he didn't know the ways of the world in this regard, and this was just the way things went. But he had been around for a bit and the strike's progress, even to someone outside of the know, seemed to be stalling a bit. Crawling would have been an appropriate term. This wasn't his baby, so he kept quiet.

More and more days were spent at the library, going through microfilms and newspaper clippings. He was finding a lot more of the same, a company mired in scandals and the occasional bailout. They were scenarios that, by themselves, were enough to crush a single small business and prevent it from ever ringing up another sale for the rest of eternity. However, when you sell enough products, and make enough money, they are mere inconveniences that happen from time to time. That's the name of the game.

He felt like he was grasping at straws as he went further back in time, but the spiral he was in was pulling him deeper. His brain had begun to see the microfilm screen when he closed his eyes. He felt his hands begin to callous from hauling texts around, feeling like he could have put on a name badge and people would have believed that he worked at that library. James felt like a man possessed, but for so long a man possessed with a dead end.

As the sun and moon came to their daily agreement to switch spots in the sky, the library's doors would soon close. Looking at one more slide for the day before he retired to a random parking lot in the area (he started staying closer to well-lit and highly trafficked areas), he saw a headline that he had yet to come across: *Ajax Automotive Out – Potrix Auto Wins Lawsuit, Will Takeover Local Plant.* Twenty-five years ago, the dateline said on the paper. This was the first time he had heard about Ajax being in the area.

Another massive corporation, Ajax Automotive was one of the biggest automotive manufacturers in the world. It had a competition with Potrix, as Pepsi had competed with Coke. Often, they weren't seen on the same turf, for reasons that anyone might expect. Often, they stayed away from one another, as there were billions of dollars for them both to make. Sometimes their paths cross though, and it could get litigious and ugly. It seemed that there was a moment of this many years ago. Before he left his job, abode, life, and all other things back in the Pacific Northwest, he remembered that Ajax and Potrix had renewed another turf war in a city only fifteen miles south as the crow flew from his work. The companies both sought a contract from the United States government to produce military-grade vehicles. He remembered reading about it in the local paper and thinking that he should start making military vehicles – he would have done it for half of what these companies would have received.

Glancing down at his watch he saw that within the hour he would be asked to leave the library to return to his wherever – it wasn't that they didn't care, but he just couldn't stay. He knew that he was going to leave that night with more questions than answers and was very annoyed that he would have been cut off from information. He thought about turning on his phone that was kept snug in the center console but remembered the promise he had made to himself.

He had moved from microfilm to the Internet and made a mental adjustment of how thoroughly he was going to look at articles for mentions of the Ajax/Potrix wars and how quickly he would move through them. He read quickly and comprehended quickly. It took him only fifteen to twenty minutes to understand how ugly the feud had become. He pored through old articles online. Rich men fighting for resources, land, capital, and labor – the American dream.

He began looking at pictures from the articles to see if any of them told a story. Most of the photos were of some suit shaking hands with someone who was probably important in circles made of money, also there were photos of assembly lines, and some dudes in sunglasses making a speech. He then came across an article about Ajax's response to losing the lawsuit. They were unhappy. They felt like the judge had been blah blah blah – the same company line that any company would have given. James rolled his eyes. But when those eyes became stationary, they landed on a half-page photo of an event outside of an Ajax factory where the CEO was giving a speech about some faux philanthropist act they were doing. Something that would look good in the moment but would just end up as a tax write-off in the end.

All The Things That Could Be

As his eyes scanned the photo, James homed in on one thing: off to the side of the photo but in focus enough to be clearly recognized was the same car that he had multiple interactions with within the town. The car was cherry red, and an older model, a model which most would have been retired to a junkyard or left in someone's yard, rotting and rusting. It was impossible to make out the license plate as it was obscured in the photo, but he felt confident in what he was looking at. He had to bring himself back to consider that the confidence was there because he wanted to believe that what he was looking at had a connection.

He drew a couple of conclusions: first, whoever owned that car had worked at Ajax but shifted their allegiance over to Potrix when the plant shifted; or, whoever owned that car was meddling in the strike. To the second point, he had to think more – why would someone from Ajax want to disrupt the strike? Ajax, if anything, would have supported it since it disrupted Potrix's bottom line. It didn't make sense, but something just did not sit right with him about it all. He had to talk to Molly about it.

He printed off the picture and moved out of the library. He wondered if he was still being watched, or if those men in the car that night figured they had scared him off. He tried to scramble all scenarios in his brain to make something make sense, each possibility seemed more outlandish than the last.

All The Things That Could Be

***

The next day, James woke early to ensure he could show his new treasure to Molly right away. The anticipation of her response made him feel giddy. He pulled up to the strike and hustled out of his car, thrusting everything in front of the labor leader.

Molly's reaction to the news was underwhelming. She didn't seem to be in a spot to make heads or tails of the information – she just took the information in at face value. James was a bit disappointed but figured that she had the strike so much on her mind that, given the time and place, he should have just waited to tell her. Her eyes darted to and fro – not from worker to worker but from location to location. James didn't know whether to push or to leave it alone, but he tried to find a middle ground. "Are you okay? Everything good?" She didn't respond. She just kept looking around.

Roland had been absent for a few days and with all the goings-on with her and James' "visits" (and who knows who else had been blessed with one), Molly was worried that a worse fate befell him. She had been on alert for three days and had tried contacting him in a couple of ways, but he was not available. No one had seen and no one had heard from him. Her fear for his safety would end up a fear for her own. The strike had drug out for a while now and there was no question that Potrix was losing significant money and potential deals. The more the strike played out, the less patient the powers that be must have been becoming, she reasoned. She was one of the vocal and visible leaders, and she didn't want to receive the Roland treatment. There were powerful forces at play.

"Bill's tonight. Normal time. We can talk." Molly murmured and then turned away. She seemed to be under the impression that she, or they, were being watched. Bill's Tavern was a union and strike den. It was the safest place she could think of.

James slinked away and headed back to his car. He checked the rearview mirror and side mirrors multiple times; he felt the eyes on him that Molly was concerned about. He never considered the limits of extrajudicial powers, but he took on Molly's worries regarding Roland. He started up the rig and drove away, trying to stay aware of his surroundings.

His curiosity brought him back to the library to explore some more about Ajax and the relationship, or lack thereof, between them and Potrix. Most of the articles he could find were rather sanitized and nothing about them gave much more insight than he already had. Then he saw it, in a section titled "Public Forum". His eyes just happened to come across it as he turned the final page. The opinion piece was from ten years ago and came from a place near Dallas. He pored over the article with great surprise, fear, relief, and a flood of other emotions. He had to make sure to check

All The Things That Could Be

himself though, sometimes those opinion pieces could be written by the wildest of characters.

Whoever wrote it put the pseudonym as "Big Bill Haywood" – so there was the possibility that the information they were giving up was so critical that they didn't feel safe to be linked to it. Ajax Automotive was being accused of putting moles into unions to work as strikebreakers or specifically to negotiate better deals for Ajax and not the workers. But it went deeper to suggest that sometimes, rarely, there were times of peace and understanding between companies, typically when labor began to get rowdy and wanted their piece of the pie. According to the unknown author, sometimes the companies will put moles into each other's union leadership, to give each company plausible deniability.

James looked away from the damning evidence and looked around unbelievingly. But he also wasn't sure if he should be so blown away by this information, and then questioned whether he should feel silly of possibility being a naif. Maybe this happened all the time, he didn't know. Either way, he felt it was prudent information. He began to reflect on the last few weeks of his time working with the strikers and tried to draw conclusions that logically fit with this new information.

He ran through all his time fighting for their cause but kept getting hung up on the meetings. The dwindling numbers, the strikebreakers – could it have been possible

All The Things That Could Be

that Roland was slow-walking the negotiations on purpose? Was that why he was missing? James countered this thought with the fact that Roland seemed to be so authentically tied to the cause. Everything was conjecture in his head, he had no reason to think anything was true and was careful to cement any of his thoughts as facts.

He took the information with him. He had printed off the opinion piece and brought it to Bill's. The amount of information he was coming with was more than he originally had, so he wasn't going to stick Molly with the same stale information as before. Perhaps, it would help. Perhaps, it would be stale as well. But for all his sleuthing, James felt as if he had dug up something that could be helpful.

The door creaked open, and Bill was busy serving a couple of locals, he gave a quick nod to James, he had grown to like him.

Chatter floated throughout the gin joint and music filled the moments when the conversations were shifting. Molly camped at a table with a full pint of beer, looking defeated. This was the first time James had ever seen her look so down and out. He wondered how best to present the information he had in a way that wasn't going to completely break her spirits.

Before he could sit down, Molly went in, "I don't think this strike is going to work. We aren't getting anywhere. We are losing the cause, losing people, losing money – we have burned through most of the relief fund and there is no end in sight. Roland has been completely gone AWOL and we have no idea where he is at. He has been bringing us through this, and now he is just gone. What are we supposed to do?"

James had settled into his seat and shuffled a little bit as he prepared to deliver. Her seeming plea for help or answers signaled to him it was an opportunity to bring theory to the table. "I think I may have some answers here. I don't know if you will love them, but they may bring clarity. But I may also have nothing at all."

Molly's head perked up as if she was hearing this for the very first time – which she may very well have been, James' words on the line from earlier went in and out. James laid out the information he had gathered, starting with the picture that contained the car, and a couple of articles about Ajax and Potrix, but he was saving the opinion piece for last, la pièce de resistance. Molly's eyes immediately took to the picture and her mouth opened and she mouthed "Oh my god."

James was thrown off by this interruption in his presentation. He wasn't sure how to handle her excitement because he hadn't even delivered what he thought would be most important. His mouth held the words in as he let her make the next decision on what they were going to talk about – but it appeared that the focus was going to be on the photo. Instead of delivering the crown jewel of information, he inquired. "Look familiar?"

All The Things That Could Be

"Yes! But how did you notice?"

"I mean, I wasn't sure, but it sounds like you're validating me in that it's definitely the same."

"Yeah, I think so. But how do you know him?"

"The car?"

"The what?"

"What are you talking about?" Both were speaking with confidence that the other one was following along, and neither of them were. James felt silly and thrust his finger in front of Molly and pointed at the classic car, one which may or may not have had a musician die in the back at some point.

Her eyes moved and widened a little bit – the dots had connected for her. She gasped. "Oh boy. Ohhhh boy. Oh boy, oh boy, oh boy." Her voice was a cocktail of panic, excitement, and bemusement. It was as if she had too much information in her head to process and a timer was about to wipe the information away if she didn't utilize it all at once. Molly's eyes darted back and forth to something else in the picture too. James finally got impatient enough to ask. "What the heck else are you looking at? Is there something else?"

"Yes! I didn't even notice the car. I thought you were talking about this guy!" Her finger lightly touched the page where a man standing among people behind the speaker. Molly turned her finger to make it very clear exactly the person she was pointing at. James didn't recognize the man;

All The Things That Could Be

he had never seen him before in his life. He looked at Molly and shrugged and waited for her to come forth with the bombshell information she seemingly had.

"This rat bastard right here is the floor supervisor in my building. He has harassed, touched, assaulted, threatened, and more to me. He is truly vile. A monster. But everybody loves him. He is super charismatic and puts on the show for everyone, only he chooses me to harass. I have no idea why. But this is definitely him." Molly was absolutely rolling the conversation. She was spitting out more words than her brain could functionally process. She was overwhelmed with excitement.

"Okay, but why is this important – so what, he moved from one company to another."

"No, no, no – this is big. Potrix and Ajax don't go back and forth like this. There are agreements in place between the two to ensure that there isn't a crossover. So, they could be breaking those rules between them, which seems unlikely, especially to waste on Heath. Or, something else is going on. I don't know what though." she pointed at the man in the photo. This felt like a big deal to James and the way Molly was rifling through the documents, he believed that he had hit on something. He let Molly bask in the information she had acquired before he laid what he now believed to be the cherry on top.

"Here is the last thing," James said calmly and slowly brought his hand from behind his back with the forum piece.

He cautioned, "Now, mind you, this is from an op-ed, so who knows how true it is or who they let write in that thing." He placed the letter in front of Molly, and she was careful not to touch it, just in case it were to catch on fire or turn to dust – she just didn't want to take the chance.

"Big Bill Haywood!" she snorted out a chuckle.

Her eyes traced left to right until she had consumed every letter.

She then read it a second time. That was a hint to James that she had found value in it.

"If this is true, this is big time." She was still looking at the paper and slowly raised her head until her eyes met James'. "If this were true, if Heath were somehow responsible for union sabotage, and this got to the Labor Board – this could be huge. Like, big time bad for both. Or one. I don't know exactly, but it could be bad." If those men from the other night only knew what they had stumbled upon now, they would have had a lot more to say than gentle identity probing.

"Do you think Roland could be a plant?" There was no easy way for James to breach this topic, he knew that Molly was fond of Roland. She remained quiet and had to process this possibility, no matter how painful it might be. James continued with his thoughts and theories. "The negotiations are going nowhere. He has slow-walked the entire thing and asked people to continue with the cause. The fund is drained and you're no closer to a deal than before. He then disappears as more people start to cross the picket line? No real leadership? Not close to a deal? What hope do you have for this right now?" In private, Roland had reneged on the work slowdown and called it off. He gave some reasoning to his inner circle, but ultimately, he said they would not take part. He called it "idealistic" and not "pragmatic".

The pieces fell together in Molly's mind. She felt like a fool for having trusted him so much. She thought it was safe to operate under that theory until something could be proved otherwise. Telling the negotiation team was important, but she also didn't know who she could trust within any circle. James and she were truly keepers of a very delicate secret. All thanks to a small, local, and now defunct newspaper.

Only a couple of years ago, the Labor Board had won a couple of Supreme Court decisions that gave a huge shift of power back towards labor – buckling down big time on the very kinds of things that were possibly in the works. To think that companies would still engage themselves in such tactics was foolish, but Heath had been at the Potrix plant for a long time. They had stayed undercover for long enough that now they must have felt veteran enough to start moving in their guise.

How far would these companies go to protect these secrets? Ajax was certainly in the know about this if their theory was true. Potrix may have been a little more difficult to finger, but you could connect enough dots to drag them into the mix. At the very least, having a mole in the plant effectively benefited them…this time. Certainly, the mole had looked to damage them, steal from them, or sabotage them in one way or another. The corporate wars were as active as any proxy war the United States was funding somewhere. All these thoughts rushed through Molly and James' heads. Where they were confused before, they were in lockstep now.

They spoke in hushed tones because they knew they could trust no one with the information they had. Molly's job was to take everything directly to the National Labor Relations Board and let them do with it what they wanted. She would heed their advice as to how to act or what to do while everything was being sorted out – hoping that they had enough evidence or leads to take them where they needed to go. She thought if they were to check in on Heath and Roland, they would probably find what they needed to, assuming Roland had disappeared for the reason they hypothesized. If they were wrong, it was going to fall on Molly, and she would have some tough times ahead.

But three weeks later when she watched a handful of executives, and Heath, get walked out of the factory by the police, she knew what they had found was worth it. And now the actual fight for a new deal could begin. As Heath left, she winked at him.

All The Things That Could Be

All The Things That Could Be

21

Sometimes when you're driving, you just get in the zone. You feel like you're driving good. It's a tough thing to describe, but it is real. Speed is right on, or at least it's in the zone where you know you're not getting pulled over and not impeding traffic.

I've been in the zone before, it feels good. The zone exists outside of driving, it's just about doing good, really good, and doing it effortlessly. The zone goes both ways, though. There also exists the other zone, the one where you work so hard, put in so much effort, and you can't even make it normal. The other zone can exist in so many different ways: economically, emotionally, physically, socially, etc.

I grew up in a family that worked hard and did well. However, that life was never given to them. My mother was a teacher and my father worked on the railroad – but these jobs had a big union presence. Dad was in one of the most recent, perhaps the most recent of all, labor battles of the twentieth century, much to Mom's chagrin. However, the unions had been robbed of their power, and that was done on purpose. The power that workers had was shrunk down, influenced by those who were the victims of worker's power. People struggled more than ever. I had an upper-middle-class job as a teacher and still struggled – financially and otherwise. I struggled partially because I saw the impacts of poverty and cronyism in so many parts of life impact the most vulnerable of people. The fight is back on, and the unions are working to take back what they deserve.

We only possess so much power as a people, one of those things is our time and our labor. Molly believed in that fight, and she helped

All The Things That Could Be

me see it through. The forces of evil are still at play, despite how many battles we win. Staying vigilant is a commitment, a lifestyle. I am committing to always fight and battle for those who don't have a system that is fighting and battling for them — but against them. I will stand and fight for people whose labor is not compensated; we must all stand up against the bloodsucking bosses who care only about profit and not the people.

May we end this reign of terror that has plagued us for so long. I will continue the fight.

-JD

22

The open road was a welcome feeling for James, and he had time to reflect on his memories with the UAW workers. Molly had taken all of the information to the NLRB, and they thought they had a real case against both Potrix and Ajax.

As a traveling man, he had learned the ways of the best amenities available to people like him. His time at the YMCAs was invaluable, as they kept him in some semblance of shape, but more importantly, clean. The libraries would be a free bastion of information where he could check the story as it continued to evolve. The time he took on the leg of the drive was substantially more than the last couple. He drove sideroads like he knew where he was going – he knew that being in the Midwest, or driving toward the northeast or New England area, he was always a gas station away from being back on track.

There was so much to see out there and many people to interact with. He would stop at stores he didn't need to shop at just to talk with people he would never see again. He would dine at restaurants he had no interest in just to yuck it up with the waiter or waitress. He continued to find people so varied and so wonderful. He thought about so many of the kids he once taught and how he worried so much for them and how they would emerge, and as he talked to so many people, he realized they would turn out just fine. Odds

All The Things That Could Be

are, they would turn out as empathetic people who were doing their best to take care of themselves and their families.

The dial on James' humanity meter was in a constant uptick on this journey. He felt like he was connecting with people in a way that he never had before. He had allowed himself to be more open with people and find the good in situations. He didn't feel constrained by the daily tragedies and worries that he once did, and the release of these things and constant worry about self, allowed him to focus on others, specifically the good in others.

His goal had been New England – somewhere, anywhere in New England. Looking at latitudinal lines, he figured that New England had to have some similar weather patterns to back home – a place he had grown to miss. He figured that he would eventually miss home, but not enough to specifically drive to a destination that simulated the area he had grown to miss. There's no place like home.

Over the last few weeks, he perused through many magazines and newspapers, looking for information about Potrix and Ajax. Both companies saw significant business in New England, specifically Delaware. While he was crushing through articles, he continuously came across advertisements for a half-marathon/marathon in Wilmington, Delaware. As he drove along the highway, the Appalachian Mountains were consuming the skyline. As fast as he drove, they barely seemed to move. It was the ultimate show of nature. Seeing this impressive form of physical geography, he pondered the idea of running a marathon. Could he do it?

. He had run recreationally for a while, so the concept of distance running wasn't foreign to him. The marathon was a month away, he would need to spend quite some time in Wilmington. He had spent significantly less money than he had anticipated and knew that he could afford lodging – sublet some apartment for a month or so, maybe a hotel. There would be things he needed to get, so the storage was important. Also, he figured it was better to rent lodging than use a YMCA shower every day for a month. At seven dollars a day, that cost was pretty equal anyway.

As he drove through those grand mountains, the AM radio tuned in and out. Sometimes complete static would envelop the song or DJ's voice, and other times it would merely linger – ready to pounce if the mountain obstructed the signal too much. The time on the road always gave him ample time to reflect on his journey and assess how he felt it was going. He was feeling extremely pleased with the adventure so far – it was more than he had hoped. But, as a man with no plan, the spectacularity could turn into problems in a flash.

Blessed with rather great luck, his car gave him no problems, his health stayed in good shape (thank you YMCA), and aside from some run-ins with death, it was relatively safe. He pontificated on how truly close to death he had been, or if he had been close at all, and wasn't able to give a real answer. He didn't know if anyone or anything that had the opportunity to take him to the next life would have. He sometimes thought about the Ajax anti-union goons and wondered if that would ever backfire on him. The less he thought about it, the less it worried him though.

Eventually, his car would roll into its destination and James scoped out a few spots to stay. He picked a cozy hotel that had a sign that emitted blue and green all night. The lobby was large enough to host multiple conferences at once, and he figured that if this place would hold that many people at once, it was because it had – it was probably safe to stay at. It had continental breakfast, and they were happy to let him stay for a month. He gave them the entire story of what he was staying there for, and a disinterested staff member along with a seemingly interested manager heard and listened – depending on which employee you were looking at.

He moved into a bed for the first time in a couple of months and it was such a nice reprieve from the car that he stayed put for a while. The race was a month away and while he didn't plan on racing it, per se, he planned on running it and giving it his best effort. He had also had to figure out where to buy shoes, running clothes, sign up for the race, and any number of things he had forgotten at that moment. Finding a store would be necessary, but not some sporting goods store that had every sport from jai alai to pickleball. He wanted to go somewhere where they knew what they were talking about. He wanted to treat himself.

All The Things That Could Be

Wilmington seemed to be more of a runner's den than he anticipated. It only took asking one person to locate the store he so sought. Much to his surprise, he was located unbelievably close to the store – walking distance was a cinch. He turned only a couple of corners, and he was face to face with marathon flyers and logos vaguely familiar to him. He knew he was in the right spot, as he looked at the ornately carved wooden sign which hung above the old brick doorframe which read "The Running Place". James didn't know if it was a reference to something in the running world, which he felt only lightly connected to, or some pop culture reference with the word "running" slipped in.

He peered through the window and didn't see anyone in the store, customer or otherwise – but the neon OPEN sign radiated a low hum he could hear a windowpane away. He pulled the door effortlessly and a bell dinged above his head, announcing his arrival. A tall, slender woman with long black braids emerged from behind a wall. She flashed a smile and tilted her head as she walked toward James. She wore jeans that canvassed her long, runner legs, and a store shirt which had two buttons on the chest, one done and one not. A golden chain hung from her luminous dark skin and the sun's light bounced off her as she moved past signs obstructing the light coming into the store. She was beauty incarnate.

"Welcome in! How can I help you?" Her melodious voice was better than any clear AM radio station he had experienced on his journey. She walked her brand new-looking running shoes right in front of him and gave him her undivided attention. He felt himself stutter and shake in a way that not even the nearness of death had made him feel. James realized he had a lot of questions and needed a lot of help, and he was glad he did.

He tried to play it cool.

"Hello. I actually have a few things. I just came into town, and I wanted to first, sign up for the marathon," he held up one finger as he began listing his needs, "or half, I'm not sure which one I should do yet, actually…" he pointed to one of the many flyers that was on the window, as if she hadn't fielded a variation of that question multiple times a week. He continued, "And I need to get some running shoes and some running clothes – shorts, shirts, socks, I suppose." After each need, another finger popped up. She nodded along with him as if she already had everything picked out that he would need.

"Yeah, we can get you set up with that. Absolutely. First, the signup." She gestured at him to the counter and floated to it while he clobbered over. She gently placed a pamphlet in his hand that had a QR code on it, as well as a place to put the information if you didn't want to do it the easy and technologically savvy way. The type of material the pamphlet was made of clearly suggested the QR code route, as you could tell any ink that ended up on it would be wet forever and would smear if merely looked at wrong.

All The Things That Could Be

James did the universal motion for a writing instrument as he bobbed from side to side with his hands acting as a second set of eyes. The associate noticed his need and gracefully supplied him with what he was looking for.

"Thank you…" He let the phrase hang like a lure in the water. He was hoping to catch a name. She bit.

"Jacie."

"Thank you, Jacie." He repeated it three times in his head to make sure it couldn't escape. He scribbled down the information, using his best penmanship – just in case Jacie was going to be the one reading it. He wanted to cause her no vexation but also wanted her to know how organized and nice he was – if she interpreted handwriting that way.

She looked at the pamphlet as a quick way to attain similar information. "Alright, James, I can get you rung up at the counter when we are all done. Now, next, you need some shoes."

The two talked back and forth about many things – James made sure to keep it running related, he didn't want to make it seem like he was trying to make small talk and flirting, he assumed she got enough of that daily. He informed her of his rather neophyte status and probed her as to her level of expertise. He could tell that she was successful in the sport, the way she looked radiated confidence: I am good at this, if you let me help you, you will be better for it. After some conversation, he found he was correct. She had been a collegiate athlete and was still training and competing in her spare time.

"Are you running in the marathon?" He inquired and hoped the answer was yes, then they could have something in common.

"Nah, I am not into marathons quite yet. I am sure I will get there eventually. But I do like to do the store runs with the training group! You should come out with us!" She beamed at the thought of being able to further help someone accomplish something. Store runs? Was that exactly what it sounded like? He hoped it was because he didn't have the faintest clue as to how to prepare for a marathon, he figured he would just run until he didn't want to run anymore for a bunch of days in a row.

"Does that cost anything?" He chose the words carefully and would have rather been seen as innocently ignorant rather than cheap.

"No. Not at all! Just a bunch of people, usually fifteen to twenty, show up three times a week for a workout. But also, we have a smaller group show up every night around the same time. The running community here really is quite nice!" Full immersion. The best way to learn the language was to be fully immersed, and that is what he planned to do. He had the luxury of a single focus – he came to run, and he could focus on just that.

All The Things That Could Be

Jacie got him squared away with some new shoes and a bunch of stuff that he wanted. He even indulged in some goods that he didn't consider before coming into the store – one of them being a new watch. Jacie said it was the best for its price, and then she flashed her watch, identical except for the color of the band. Immediately, he wanted a band that complimented hers. The wanton spending of money may have been a clue that he wasn't broke. James couldn't believe he was having all of these subconscious thoughts about his actions; it made him wonder if he was purchasing functionality or to impress.

He held in his hands everything that he needed and caught a glimpse of himself in the mirror. His reflection made him look like someone who had never run before in his life, or a sucker who had just bought a ton of products to impress someone, or maybe both. In his mind, he shrugged it off. He was registered for a full marathon (he had been talked into it, but she could have convinced him to run a 100 miler and he would said yes) and had plenty of gear to go home and try on, lace up, charge, put on, configure…the list went on. But he felt a little bit like he did on any given Christmas of his youth. These were exciting times!

Before he left the store, he managed to get information about the running group that met three days a week. He brought up the other running group that Jacie had mentioned and asked if that was for someone new to the scene. She let him know it wasn't a problem, but it also wasn't very structured – a bit of a choose-your-own-adventure. He thanked her and made sure to say her name one more time before he left.

A smile captured the face of James as he moseyed his way back to the hotel room. He came through the lobby doors and made sure to greet his housemates for the next month. Up the elevator he would ride, and, in his temporary home, he began taking off tags, lacing up shoes, charging the watch, and putting on the different sets of tops and bottoms to see what went best together. He caught himself during his excitement and laughed. He had been so unbothered by the ways of the world lately that he felt as if he were reverting to a more carefree state.

Before he knew it, he might have been passing notes that ended with: If You Like Me, Check Yes.

23

She lined up on the starting line of the National Championships for the 1500-meter run. The nerves of the day, week, year, and collegiate career, were all extinguished in a moment when the gun fired – a signal for the gladiators to begin their battle in the arena. She sprinted into position, right in the middle of the field. Aligning her position in the pack with her game plan for the race. She was only 150 meters into the race when one of the racers' stride entangled with her own. The first thought in her mind was the only thought she had until she crashed to the ground: oh no.

Jacie and the other girl tumbled to the ground, after trying to save their fall to no avail. In the attempt, Jacie's foot landed on the inner rail and rolled off violently. Pain ripped through her foot and ankle as she skidded to a halt right there on the track. The other half of the collision fared better, she got back up and managed to claw her way back into 7th place.

Rolling off the track, literally, and into the infield, she prayed that the javelin was being thrown and that she would be impaled by a weapon of war. So much work, sweat, and time sacrificed – all of it to end no more than twenty-five seconds into the race. She was heartbroken and disappointed – but mostly she was embarrassed and ashamed. She knew what her coach would say - that it wasn't her fault and there was no reason to feel that way. But she knew that he knew that those words would act as little solace for her broken heart and possibly broken ankle.

Occasionally, Jacie would wake up in the middle of the night and her ankle would hurt. As time marched on, the wake-ups would be less and less frequent, but now and again it would still happen. She believed the pain to be in her head, parked right next to the "what-ifs" and regret. She felt foolish for living in the past for so long, but she blamed this on being competitive.

After college, Jacie bounced around from job to job for a while before abandoning the idea of being a lifelong corporate white-collar worker for good. She had told her friends and family that those places had no soul.

A possible connection opened for Jacie when a college teammate reached out to her some seven years ago. "My parents own a running store in Wilmington, but they want to retire and move down south. Would you be interested in buying it from them?" Jacie had saved money like a miser, lived at home, and did little in her free time but run and read. She had the opportunity, but it was an investment that she wasn't sure would pan out. True, she would come in with an established customer base, well, she hoped. She considered the offer and did some research on the opportunity.

Her family was very supportive of buying the store. They emphasized her hatred of corporate America for the lack of soul and owning this store could allow her to interject her soul into somewhere people would want to be. She could spread her love of sport, and hopefully encourage people to join the sport that she so much enjoyed. She remembered a quote from one of her favorites in running coaches "There are three things you can never have back: First is time, the next is spoken word, and last is opportunity." This was an opportunity that if she passed by, she may never be able to get back. She would, no doubt, drain most of her savings (if not all of it) to make this dream a reality. But, what else would the money be for? She decided that she would.

The sale and takeover seemed to sneak up on her. Before she knew it, Jacie was moving out to Wilmington, where she had rented an apartment near the shop. The previous owners went out of their way to ensure the store looked nice. They had taken down the old sign, one of the few changes that Jacie wanted to ensure. Since it was no longer the "Hamilton Family Running Shop" (a peculiar name to begin with), and she certainly was not a Hamilton, the name had to go.

The name she had in mind came as a knockoff from the Splash Mountain ride, which had a section known as "The Laughing Place". It may not have been the most creative name in the world, but for some reason it made her laugh and things that made her laugh were her favorite things.

She was familiar with the process and how much it would take to get the shop back off the ground. There was so much to do – inspections to be done, papers to file, contracts to re-secure, there was no end to getting something like this up and running. The hours turned into days and the days into weeks – there always seemed to be some hang-up, something that wasn't filed – or not filed correctly. Jacie spent no shortage of hours at the store – she did most of her nuts and bolts work in the store, getting a feeling for it, and beginning to inject some soul into the building.

Time and again she would have people come by the store, cup their hands, and peer into the window. Whether they were old customers waiting for the revival of their favorite store or just curious citizens was always a question that Jacie wondered. Sometimes she would go to engage the curious, sometimes they would scamper off and other times she would be wrapped up in a conversation that went longer than she anticipated – but she appreciated it. She wanted to connect with the tenets of the city be a friendly face, and hopefully find a place to spend money or join a new hobby.

Her parents would occasionally come out to help with small things, or just to gaze upon their daughter's accomplishment and bathe in the pride they felt. For the opening day, they held a store party where many of Jacie's immediate and extended family came out to celebrate, and a few of her high school and college teammates found their way to the store as well. A few members of the community visited on the first day and got to know the new owner. The number of people who ended up in the store excited Jacie and surprised her a bit – she ran out of 10% off coupons she had created for the anticipated crowd. No one seemed to mind because the food and drink were delicious and never ran out.

***

The first week was a bit slower than she had anticipated based on the first-day party. Her traffic was relatively low, and she wondered if she was going to need to have three extra employees or if she was going to need to cut back already. The thought of it stressed her out and she bounced between thoughts of "this is common for new businesses" and "I wonder if I was sold something that was already dying."

Saturday night came and went, the numbers for the first week did not jump out at her and she thought she may have to dip further into her savings to keep this store afloat. She left the store after eight in the evening. She turned the key and locked the store as she heard the beeping of the alarm system arming itself. She pulled her hood on her head and turned into the cold rain and headed back toward her apartment. Once she got home, she kicked off her shoes and changed into her pajamas where she would sulk in her couch for the rest of the night.

All The Things That Could Be

***

Jacie's phone erupted at two in the morning. She fumbled around trying to comprehend the situation of why someone was trying to get in touch with her at such a god-awful hour.

"Uh, hello? Hi? Hello?" She answered the phone and wondered if she was too late to answer.

"Hello, this is Paul from AIT Security. We have received a report that your alarm has been set off. Would you like us to send police?"

She woke up quickly after hearing this and was now very present and very sober feeling. Operating in total clarity. But she settled and thought there was a simpler answer to the question at hand. "Um, no thank you. I live close to the store. I will go take a look."

She found the clothes that she had peeled off just a few hours ago but found a heavier jacket and made her way out of her apartment. She hustled down the stairs and took a quick walk to the store. The streetlights projected the precipitation and the wind – both had calmed down significantly from the last time she was out and about, but they were still hanging around. As she turned down the street, her eye caught a million tiny reflections on the ground as a car drove down the street toward her. The front window of her store had been completely shattered.

All The Things That Could Be

Instant stress. She hurried to the store to find everything still inside – she had not been looted, but a brick lay near the running mannequin, who seemed rather unbothered by the entire affair. Her hands met her face as she pulled down on her cheeks and said, "Oh my god." There was glass everywhere, a brick on the ground, and a lot of questions to be answered. She turned on the light and put in the code to extinguish the silent alarm, then took out her phone and called the police. Their interest seemed sleepy, but they said they would send someone out.

She didn't even know where to begin or what to do, so she did nothing. She stood in her store as the rain and wind occasionally shifted and blew into the store. She turned around to go into the back and check the inventory, to make sure the product and the safe were still there. When she did, she noticed another addition to the store, this time it was on the front counter. Spray painted in red over some autographed posters by some track legends was a message "Time to Leave!!" book-ended by swastikas.

Behind her, she then heard, "Ah jeez." She turned around and saw the police officer's face squeezed into frustration and exasperation. "Not this again."

24

Jacie stayed in the store all night, giving a statement, talking with the officer, and figuring out what to do with the window – short-term and long-term. The officer informed her that there had been an uptick in racial violence lately – an acting Pennsylvanian white supremacist group was branching into Delaware and, lucky them, it was taking place around Wilmington. The group had calmed down for a bit, but it looked like they were still out there. Jacie gave him all the information that she could think of which may have helped him out. She knew that nothing she said would be enough to identify someone involved and enable the officer to hop in his car and take down the ring, but she told the story as if it could.

"If I had to take a guess, some of those people who attended your first-day celebration weren't there because they wanted to run a 5k anytime soon." Jacie was sickened by the image brought up by the comment.

Was this what she was going to have to contend with? A threat to her life anytime she opened her store or closed it? She thought about calling her parents, but she needed time to process the whole scenario. Sundays weren't days that she was open, so she just spent the rest of the day sweeping up glass, boarding up the window, scrubbing the spray paint off the counter, and planning her next move.

All The Things That Could Be

Eventually, she did call her parents and let them know that she was okay, but what had happened. Her father and mother were irate, and they jumped into the car and were there in a concerningly fast time.

As they came through the door, Jacie spun and saw them. With tears in her eyes, obscuring her vision, she guessed her way over to them and melted into their hold. She felt as long as she was being held by them, no one could hurt her. She was probably right. Her father was intimidatingly large, and her mother was a small frame, but she had done incredible feats of strength in her life. As they held her, her father could still see the message, despite the attempted scrubbing. He rubbed her head and said, "Baby, you're gonna need some paint."

The family worked all day getting the store back into some semblance of shape and ready for Monday. Even so, when they left for the evening, the store still looked as if it were feeling the wound of the attack. Jacie called the insurance company and scheduled a time for a window replacement, called the police, and had to nearly beg for them to say they would send someone near the store on a more consistent basis. They also told her they had no new information and were no closer to catching the perpetrator of the crime. They assured her that they were doing all they could to find out who was responsible, however.

Jacie's parents stayed in her small apartment and comforted her. This was not the first time the family had dealt with racist taunting and harassment, but it was the first time that Jacie had been such a target. She expressed her fear, now regret, about owning the store, but both her parents were resolute about not giving up because of cowards. They had always instilled a sense of pride in her about who she was, and they also told her the history of what their people had endured. She knew it wasn't a pretty story, but they were resilient people, and they stayed resilient by standing up.

The next day, the three left the apartment early to head to the store. Her father was going to stay and ensure the glasswork got done and her mother was going to help around the store however she could – a jack of all trades. The morning sky was speckled with patches of blue sky, otherwise covered by mildly threatening clouds. Poker face clouds – were they going to give up the tell or not? The weather report was as confused as anyone, as the predictions kept changing. A chill carried through the air and reached anyone who stepped out of their abodes.

The short walk was refreshing, but that refreshment turned to anxiety when they turned the corner. The street which "The Running Place" was on was packed with diesel trucks sporting massive American flags, Second Amendment stickers (Come and Take It), cars and SUVs with similar messages, vehicles with Pan-African flags on them, one car had a Malcolm X sticker, another with a Black Panther quote, and Jacie even thought she saw Marcus Garvey there.

All The Things That Could Be

The family slowed, stopped, and looked at each other to see if any of them had received an email or text message which would have explained this with simplicity. The street couldn't fit another car, it was like a parade had accidentally ended up on her store's street. Jacie didn't know whether to make heads or tails (or both) of the incident and immediately considered if it was going to impact her business day. She knew that almost every car she saw with a symbol on it could make someone feel uneasy. They moved cautiously toward the throng and realized that the occupants of those vehicles were crowding the sidewalk, including directly in front of her store.

From a distance, she was immediately able to see four men with AR-15s standing, with gaffers covering their mouths, still as if they were on guard of something. There was an instinct to turn and run, but they were noticed, and nothing had changed, so they must have been safe enough. They walked toward the scattered crowd with curiosity and less anxiety than before, as it had turned into confusion. She saw three bulky and scruffy-looking men removing the wood that she had boarded up her shop with, while other men looked on, some enjoying what looked and smelled like coffee.

With her mother and father on her side, she approached the men and nervously said, "Hello? Can I help you?"

A short man with a thick mustache emerged as the vocal leader with zero hesitation. "Are you the owner of this business?" He was straight to the point and seemed to have little patience when asking the question.

"Yes, yes, I am. You are taking down the board that I had to repair my shop with yesterday." Jacie shot back in a tone that matched this mustachioed and tattooed man.

"We heard what happened. And I can tell you, that ain't gonna happen again." Jacie looked at her dad and then back to the man. "Excuse me?"

"We heard you were visited by some skinheads – they have been giving Wilmington a run for a bit now. Well, we got sick of it. All of us are volunteers who look to stomp out that nonsense. We protect our community and sometimes handle things the way we see fit."

The men had pried the boards off and four other men walked over a large pane of glass and they began to set it. Her eyes watched the men unbelievably.

"Yeah. We have been here for a while. Darnell is the guy who would have taken the insurance job – if you have called that claim, cancel it. We got this covered. Coffee?" He gestured to the three.

One of the men was talking to the four gun-toting statues and then walked over to the family. "I am sorry that you must deal with this. Name's Clement." He stuck out his large mahogany hand. He shook the hands of everyone and

All The Things That Could Be

then got back to business, "This is Skip. These are all our boys here – you can think of us as an…equal rights enforcement unit if you will. Equal rights for all – that means the right to equally feel safe." Jacie had to admit that at the first cross-street she walked to, safe was not the word she would have landed on, but as she took in the whole scenario, she realized that this was an odd feeling of safety and security. There were a lot of things that made her feel a little worrisome as she came down the street (her parents equally so), but now she realized their intent and their mission had transcended any message that she had originally assumed.

"With your permission, we will have our sentry over here post up over the next week. We will rotate guys in and out, but like Skip said, we will ensure the protection of our fellow citizens." Clement gave the speech with such coolness and normalcy; it was like he was talking about an old family story that everyone had heard a hundred times. Jacie had not considered this to be a possibility when she opened "The Running Place" – she scanned the files in her brain to find out what the business owner's manual said about an armed guard to combat Neo-Nazis. Nothing!

"Uh, um, I mean, yes. Yes, I think that is fine. But, well, I don't know, what about my customers? They…" her hesitancy was anticipated by Clement, and he already had the answer.

"Your customers won't be impacted. Not in a negative way. People know who we are, and they know what we do." Jacie's head whipped back and forth to her mother and father looking for the nod of a head or shake of disapproval, like she was asking to spend the night at a friend's house on a school night. They smiled and reminded her that this was her decision to make, not theirs.

"Yes. Thank you. What will it cost?" Jacie braced for the number coming. Security was worth the cost if it kept the bad at bay.

The Skip character laughed and waved a piece of paper in front of their faces, "I am already getting ten percent off my next purchase. What more can we ask for?" He laughed more and then Clement cut in, "There is no cost. This is something we do for people. We are covered, financially. We just want to make sure our people are taken care of."

A single tear welled in Jacie's eye. She was moved by the kindness of everyone. Behind her, he heard her father laugh and said, "Man, I'm gonna go home get mine, and show up!" Jacie heard her mother smack his arm and retort, "Like hell you are."

Jacie opened the store, and the windowpane was installed. She canceled the insurance claim.

The group brought in a bunch of food and drink and set it up in the store. Her mother and father made the rounds and talked to every single one of the helpers, expressing their gratitude. Figuring out who was a parent in the conversation was obvious. The group said it was their duty to battle against such hate. No one inquired as to what their definition of "battle" entailed, but sometimes you don't need to know the specifics of every extrajudicial group out there.

The entire week, the storefront found four armed men occupying the sidewalk – Jacie rarely saw them move, but knew they talked back and forth to one another. Their discipline was impressive – she often offered them food and coffee. For men with faces covered for protection and wielding weapons of war, they were quite polite. The entire week also saw a large uptick in business. The customers were completely unbothered by the group out front, but they also didn't stick around to talk to them – it was like the customers understood the job they did. Everyone seemed to be in the know.

The store was busy all week and the trepidation Jacie had only a week before about money had evaporated. She was gathering a customer base at a rapid rate and knew they would be repeat customers. Skip and Clement's group had some pull in the community, the increased traffic could not have just happened by chance. Initially, she wanted to bring running and joy into the community, but now she wanted to make sure she was doing something to better the lives of its residents. She wouldn't be fighting skinheads as a side hustle, but she could do something else to bring people together. She started putting out the feelers for two things: the first was a marathon in Wilmington, and the second was using the store as a meeting place for local runners to meet up and run together.

The feedback she received on both issues was met with excitement and some people expressed something that sounded like a need to have these things. Jacie was overwhelmed by how things turned so quickly in her favor. Later in the week, the police officer who she had called the night of the vandalism stopped by. Jacie had put two and two together and figured he had to of been the one who contacted Clement or Skip and let them know what happened. "I have to thank you for everything." Jacie motioned around her.

The officer gave a questionable look, understanding what she was referencing, and said, "It would be unbecoming and unprofessional, dangerous even, of an officer of the law to encourage vigilante justice." His face was cold and stern, almost a look of disgust that she would suggest he recommend such. He held the look for what seemed like a minute but was much shorter. Then he smiled. "So, we will keep looking and keep our eyes peeled. If anything new happens, please let us know."

He turned and left out the door, discreetly fist-bumping one of the guards along the way.

Two days later a man with an "88" tattoo on his neck was found dead in a ravine near the border of Pennsylvania and Delaware. The murder is still unsolved.

All The Things That Could Be

25

James had a couple of hours to waste before the meetup, he planned on getting there fifteen minutes before, since he understood it as unofficial, sometimes those times are plus or minus some minutes. He was excited about this new endeavor and had committed in his mind to doing the best he could. He would commit to running every day – if that is what people did at least. He remembered that was a question he would need to ask someone who knew more than him, and hopefully whose name was Jacie.

Smitten.

He then curbed his excitement – he knew nothing about her. She could have been married, uninterested, or both, for all he knew. Didn't want to put the cart ahead of the horse. Well, not more than he already had.

He dawdled until it was time for him to make his way over to the store to run. Once he got there, he didn't know the protocol or what to do while waiting. Did they meet in the store or outside of it? He didn't want to loiter and look like a weirdo in the store, but he also wasn't sure if his presence just outside the store was any better. So, he did what he thought communicated the most innocuous message, he started just doing some stretches. He wasn't even sure if they were the right stretches, but they seemed to be helping. He wasn't sure. He wasn't even focused on whether the stretch was warming up the right muscle group or not, James was focused on looking busy. He looked around to see if he could find anyone who might fit the descriptor of "runs at unofficial running store get-togethers", but no one, and perhaps everyone, seemed to fit that build.

Much to his surprise and pleasure, a warm voice behind him caught his attention. "You are a little early, this group is often a bit slow to get going. Do you want to come on in here? They typically meet in the store." Jacie's invitation was welcomed, and he stepped inside wearing only things that Jacie had sold him a few hours before.

Inside the store, a warm environment of fellowship enveloped the mood. A television showed a track meet happening somewhere, a customer was trying on shoes with the help of another employee – the store just felt…safe. He wasn't even a runner runner. Not like those you see day in, and day out, on top of all of the new training trends, with the newest and fastest shoes, signing up for all the races all the time, posting it on their social media as soon as they cross the finish line. He wasn't like that – he wasn't that definition of a runner, his definition. But all the same, he felt like he didn't need to be. Even when he had dabbled in the sport before, he felt like he got points simply for trying – it was a grace that he always afforded to others.

The weather began to change, and it would obscure the windows. James looked from side to side to see if anyone else was concerned with how quickly and foreboding the fog had rolled in. No one seemed to care, so he continued to plod around the store and wait for whomever he was waiting for. Jacie was helping another man, who looked like he knew what he was doing when it came to the sport, so he didn't try and battle for her attention.

A couple of harriers walked through the door; these must have been his new people. He walked over as they mingled and introduced himself. While he was shaking hands with the potential new friends, a few more walked through the door, and he knew he was in good company. The small group ranged all ages, but the jovial nature infected them all. James began chatting with someone his senior, a man in his late fifties, shorter, skin made up of many pictures and colors and a black mustache that jutted out from his face. The men exchanged basic information – the tattooed man's name was Rafi, but everyone just called him Skip.

Skip had been a longtime customer of the store and a longtime resident of the city. He was a steelworker who found solace in pounding pavement on the open road. He was a veteran of the marathon, despite not being too fast. His muscles and joints ached and groaned from the work he did, he accepted his occupation would render his body slower, so he never tried to go above and beyond what his legs thought they could achieve without too much stress.

As a couple more people trickled into the store, the inclusive nature only seemed to increase. James introduced himself to most of the group but found himself back chatting with Skip. He gave him the easy version of where he was from and what he was doing – but he didn't go into details about what he had already done. The steelman looked at him like he had some youthful foolishness that was driving this adventure – a fact not false. "That is quite the tale there." A statement that had a touch of patronization about it, but James understood that the idea was inane to many. Many people were so entrapped by the ways their lives were structured for them around those forty to fifty hours a week in which they had to perform to survive.

The run was a five-mile loop that zigged and zagged through local neighborhoods, according to Jacie, who had come out of the back, ready to run. "Ah, Jacie doesn't usually join these runs – we must be blessed tonight," Skip said above the crowd, a laugh was repaid for his words. "Someone has to make sure you don't get into too much trouble out there, Skip. Besides, we got a new person today – thought I'd be a good host." James blushed – because he was pretty sure she was talking about him.

Jacie, James, and Skip trotted along a paved trail which was made for which they were using it, the trail was there in part because of some serious lobbying that Jacie had been a part of. James probed into the nature of the town and tried to get a feel for where he was staying. He listened intently as they ran, and then sometimes took a walk break – of the three, none of them knew who the walk breaks were actually for – James thought they may have been for Skip since he was a bit older; Jacie and Skip thought they were for James, who was the new kid on the block.

By the last mile of the run, the sky was black except for the lights of cars and buildings. The sounds of commuters making their way home were made from a distance. James asked the two about the marathon and what advice they had. He informed them of his intent to train as much as he could, as he really didn't have too much else going on at this point in his life. They offered the advice they could. Skip was running the marathon as well, as he always did, and James thought perhaps they could run it together. But he didn't know if that was crossing too much runner etiquette to suggest that so soon. That could have been like proposing on the first date but in running language.

They trotted back to the store and hung around talking for a while before Skip excused himself, leaving Jacie and James alone to chat. James stayed until closing before he bid the storeowner goodnight and headed back to his hotel.

***

Days passed by and James felt the strength of running in his legs, typically in the form of tiredness and exhaustion, but he knew those were code terms for "getting better". The hotel he was staying at had an exercise room with the weights he had been accustomed to, like those at the YMCA. He also loved not having to shower and get ready in their locker rooms, not that he didn't appreciate them, but the privacy now was a highlight.

Whether running with the marathon squad or running with the people who just showed up, James had taken a liking to Skip and often tried to meander his way into his periphery. Everyone in the group was fine enough, some people tried to give James unwarranted advice from time to time, and while it was surely given with the best intentions, it got obnoxious. He tried to stay away from those, and Skip certainly wasn't one of them. He only advised if James asked for it, and he did ask Skip quite a bit.

As they ran through the town and on the different routes that had been carved out by the running community, Skip would point out different parts of the city. Where events happened or where a dead president had once spilled coffee on himself. James eventually learned about the "group of friends" that had come to intervene on Jacie's behalf when she first opened the store. "No, we don't have a name, that just makes it hokey. We just...do." The group was one of the most interesting things that James had ever heard about. He had never thought something like this was possible in the Pacific Northwest, but out here in the American Old World, things must have worked a little differently.

"Do you ever worry about becoming a target?" James asked midstride as they crossed through a park.

All The Things That Could Be

"I don't have time to worry about things like that. We don't want some turf war. Let me correct myself," Skip looked at James as their stride synced up, "they don't want some turf war. We are just fed up."

James probed about the group a bit more and was satiated with the amount of information he received before he potentially could have tripped a line of annoyance with Skip.

"That is some of the coolest stuff I have ever heard, Skip. I tip my hat to you." James paid the compliment.

"I wish we didn't have to be at all." Skip lamented the existence.

***

The weather in the northeast was like a little touch of home for James. The leaves were fully vacated from their trees, the parks looked cold, wet, and barren. Rain blessed the grounds multiple times a week, but it never seemed to deter the runners – a group that James had been accepted into and had become very fond of. He had been to at least five different member's houses for dinner or general frivolity. The group had found him and his journey incredibly interesting and they often inquired about what "this" state was like, or what "that" city had to offer.

All The Things That Could Be

    James was working on making inroads with Jacie as well. One night, staying late at the store, he inquired about taking her to see a movie – a request that was agreeable to her. Not wanting to make it seem like too big of a deal, though it was to him in his head, he suggested just heading over after work, if that, too, was agreeable of course. It was. She was excited about the prospect of continuing to get to know him on a better level, what they knew about one another did not go too deep, after all.

    At the theater, they both agreed to an old cult classic that was appearing back on the big screen either because it was some anniversary celebration or because the theater owners appreciated said film and wanted to give the commoner a look at what they perceived as culture. The theater acted as a venue for them to meet up and the movie was used as a medium to conduct conversation through – it was a timer, one that gave them an excuse to sit next to each other and converse about everything. The timer began with trivia and previews and ended up with credits – no one else inhabited the theater room so they were free to break the rules of common courtesy.

    James further clued Jacie into his cross-country road trip and how he'd been on the journey for a couple of months at that point. He talked about the circumstances he had got himself into and the trouble he had found. He told her about the strike and the time at the gas station. About the deer he almost impaled with his car and how he ended up turning around on the highway late at night. About the diner that had been evacuated when he was in it, and the haunted parking lot he was convinced he stayed in. Jacie hung on every word and wasn't sure if she should like him more for all the stories he had or show him disdain for the insane stories he might be making up for clout. Each story had her reevaluating her feelings and the reality that these stories truly happened. In the end, she decided these stories would have been silly to make up, and would have been very weird to sit around and plan them, which made her then think, "Is this man some weird sociopath playing the long con?" A spiral of thoughts that she could have drowned in for the rest of the night if she let herself do it. So, she stopped.

James finally got to a point of embarrassment because he realized how much he had been talking. He abruptly threw on the brakes and tried to organically shift the conversation toward Jacie. He truly was more intrigued about her than he was in his journey, but he realized how much his journey had brought him. He implored her to do what he had just done as to even the scoreboard. There was no shortage of accomplishments that she could talk about that would impress him to no end. She was a modest woman, however, and even though she was fully aware of how awestruck he was right to be about who she was and how hard she worked to get there, she pulled back the reigns significantly. Maybe one day.

She did give him a little bit of background though and told him about her athletic prowess, specifically in the terms of her training – and how much joy it brought her. She appreciated structure and she thrived on the rigidity of her coaches. Expectations were set and expectations were achieved. Not that she thrived on any external stimuli, but merely the fact that she accomplished something difficult. The best things in her life had been found in delayed gratification, perhaps it was why she was attracted to James. He lived in a world that she felt had no oxygen, full of things she only wanted to see from afar. She was impressed with his ability to pick up his life and just leave. She was in awe of his commitment to uncertainty; he appreciated her commitment to structure.

As soon as the previews began, the credits rolled. Their time had been extinguished in an instant, an instant that resulted in one knowing much more about the other than when they had come in – it was the deal they made when they entered the venue of time and conversation. As they shuffled around their seats, getting ready to allow the workers to come in and clean up the mess they hadn't made, Jacie's hand grazed James' face. In an instant, James was teleported home – but home existed as a feeling of safety, security, and love, not as a wooden structure on a street corner. Never a place that he could drive to, but only a place that someone could take him to. He grasped the armrest to stabilize himself and his head crossed the threshold of seat space and then that of personal space. The two closed their eyes but still managed to meet like two puzzle pieces – perfectly together.

All The Things That Could Be

26

The morning of the marathon came quickly. James had done all the safe preparation tips he had picked up from the store, which had a pre-race meal get-together for any of the training group members who wanted to show up. He got dressed and made his way to the festivities – he was aware that this was not simply going to be a race for some and run for others, but a moment of pride for Wilmington runners and the general populace. As he stepped outside of the hotel doors, the crisp, cold air broke into his lungs with force. He was nearly knocked back into the hotel doors by it. He regained his composure and pulled his hood over his ears. "Lord almighty." He breathed into his hands.

Snow wasn't in the forecast but no one who was at the race that day would have bet the house on it. As James moved around the city streets, he saw food trucks being set up, and city workers directing traffic – including workers hoisting the truss for the finish line. A clock was hung on the truss and red eights streamed across the display. It was so cold that it impeded conversation, most people had their faces buried into a jacket or gaffer, trying to keep their chins tucked into their chests.

Many runners, including James, were smart enough to know that these things would change, perhaps not with time, but certainly with movement. As he started to move and run around, he would warm up. Everyone at the race would have the same instinctual thought: I should overdress. And those who listened to that thought would certainly regret it.

As he worked his way toward the store, he was surprised to see that Jacie was already inside. He felt like he had enough relationship capital to knock on the window in the hopes of being let in. The knock took its toll, hurting his knuckle from the cold, but her warm reception to the knock took away the pain instantly. The lock clicked as Jacie opened the door and a rush of warm air pulled James into the store. The entire city's cold air tried to force its way into the warmth, but Jacie's strength and resolve got the door shut and locked again. "Lord almighty." exclaimed the store owner.

"This should be no problem for you! You told me you trained in colder…for longer!" James was proud to bring out the information that Jacie had blessed him with in that sanctuary of time. Jacie smirked and appreciated the effort. "There is a big difference between training in the cold and just existing in it. Anyway, I have become soft over time." She joked with him and then something clicked in her head, and she spoke in rapid fire, as if she spoke too slowly then she would forget. "My parents called me last night and they decided they are coming out this morning." James wanted to interpret the message as "I want you to meet my parents because I like you" but realized that was a bold assumption to make, so he played it safe, "Oh that's great! I hope I get the chance to meet them." He wasn't sure if he played it off as cool as he thought.

She cracked him a look over her shoulder and his braids danced from the front of her body to the back, "Yeah, well, I would hope so." She laughed. James felt confident but didn't want to set himself up for disappointment.

"Which brings me to a good point," she slowly turned around and placed his hands on her hips, "what's the plan with this? What are we doing? What is your plan after Wilmington? Is this your last day?" The two of them had talked briefly about James' plans after the marathon, he had considered spending another chunk of cash to stay at the hotel for a little longer. It would be a lie to say it wasn't mostly influenced by Jacie's presence. He would have spent every cent he had if it meant hanging out with her.

"Yeah, I don't know. I mean – I would like to see where this goes. Jacie, I am a nomad. I could go back to Washington, but there is as much there for me as there is anywhere." Her eyes flashed at him quickly as if he had gravely omitted something. "Except here!" He rescued the answer.

"Damn right, boy." Her confidence was certainly in the top one hundred things he liked most about her. "Well, you're going to meet my parents and they know a little bit about you. Just be you and you'll be fine." She sounded like she was guiding him through the process, and he knew he would end up safely on the other side. James nodded and felt as if he was transported home.

The sun rose slowly behind the clouds and the streets began to come into full view. People were meandering here and there. Each minute that passed saw more people enter the area, many of them adorned in running garb, but some spectators – dressed to the nines with warm clothes –were even bearing signs of support. James didn't know what to expect – he had gleaned information and insight into what it may look like, but some of that information was conflicting. He had wondered if everyone would show up ten minutes before and gridlock the area, or if people would trickle in hours before to just hang around. He had wondered if people would be running around and getting warmed up hours beforehand, or if there would be, unrecognized by him, Olympic hopefuls shuffling anonymously throughout the crowd – sipping their coffee and mentally preparing for the long road ahead.

James chatted with Jacie for a few minutes but realized that this was a big business day for her, so he asked if there was anything he could do to help. She dismissed him without his help and told him where the group would be meeting up. "Who are you running with again? Skip?" She paid attention to detail – it was something that she knew people valued. It helped in her personal life, and it also helped continue revenue streams into the store.

"Yup. I'll be out there trying to hang with the old boy." He responded.

"I think you'll be fine. Just make sure you have fun. I'll see you at the end." She took her hand to her lips and then sent him a note of love and luck throughout the air. He reached out and caught it – as corny as the gesture was, he felt as if he didn't have a choice. She laughed.

She led him back outside and he moved to the rally point of the team. They were all huddled about waiting for the meeting to officially begin as determined by the clock, not the members. It was too cold to be late. James felt relief that he wasn't the last of the group to join, he buried his hands in his pockets like the rest of them and breathed into his zipper. "Great day for racing!" Someone in the group observed, and while it sounded like a crazy statement at the moment, they all knew it was better than heat.

The group got their numbers and decorated their shirts with them. They ran around a little bit, up and down streets, and each street brought about the realization that being cold was just a temporary state of being. They had crossed into a threshold that didn't exist for people who weren't running at that moment. They lived in the same world but in two different existences.

Skip and James warmed up, running around and looking at the thousands of harriers who descended on the city for the sole purpose of hours of running. Touring the streets, they noticed that the lower the number on the bib, the more the person resembled a modern-day Adonis. They even witnessed the first bib executing his pre-race routine, resembling a quiet confidence while looking like pure muscle. James stole a glance at the name and wondered how "Kristoffer" would perform on that day. He wondered what it was like for him in the middle of the race. Did he suffer like a normal person? Was it easy for him? Did he suffer more because he ran faster? Was he merely a conduit of suffering because he could handle it?

The pair got down to their racing attire and moved toward the checkerboard line that had been painted across the roadway. The crowd descended upon the starting line like locus upon a field. A woman gave instructions on the loudspeaker, but no one could hear over the hundreds of small conversations that were happening in the area. Additionally, those who weren't talking were in their own head, detailing their plan for survival of such a momentous task.

A voice came over them, different from that of the one on the loudspeaker. A man at the front barked orders in a way that commanded the attention of everyone. The street was lined with spectators yelling, cheering, and waving. Police lights flashed like a rave down the street, blocking cross-streets – today belonged to the runner. A flash in the air followed by a loud bang and the runners were off. Some were patient to leave their position while others acted as if they were in Pamplona and the bulls were just released.

All The Things That Could Be

The pair of men engaged in a more moderate action, running forward but without such urgency and without the seeming peril that other runners felt. James was able to keep pace with Skip, as he thought he would be able to, he was significantly younger than Skip and thus the training took to him a bit easier than Skip's did. There were times during the race when he felt he could have overtaken Skip and buried him. James wondered if Skip was thinking the same thing – that perhaps neither of the men were hurting too bad and both were holding back for the sake of the other. It would have been quite embarrassing to try and speed up and leave Skip only to find out that he was being pleasant, and then turn the tables on him. Then, if that did happen, how that would look at the finish line having a conversation about it? The risk outweighed the reward and he decided against it.

Wilmington was a marathon destination, there was no doubt about it. James had briefly seen some bigger venues for marathons and believed this went right up there with any of them. Every street he sped down was packed with supporters and dreamers – people enraptured with the thought of "next year, that will be me out there!" without considering the training that it would take them to get there. Not that James or Skip believed that anyone was looking at them and making them the standard, but the people who were quite possibly handcrafted by God to ensure they could take on such endeavors. Direct descendants of Job himself, truly able to harbor any pain and torment put upon them.

All The Things That Could Be

The idea of work culminating in a specific goal was never lost on James and certainly wasn't a new phenomenon, but going from struggling through 40 minutes of running to successfully completing an eighteen-mile run and still smiling at the end emphasized the idea. The process was the focus, and the product was a bonus. Surely, this was not a universal creed, and perhaps it fluctuated from activity to activity, or from person to person, but it was sticking with James. If he could focus on and appreciate the journey, rather than the result, maybe he could find more inner peace in more parts of his life. That philosophy seemed to sink more and more into his soul with each step he took, so much so that he felt like he wanted to ask Skip about it, but as he opened his mouth he was brought back to earth and reminded that he was a lot more tired than he had anticipated. Trying to have a full-blown conversation at that point would have been the death knell to his own race, and if Skip felt anything like he did when he opened his mouth, the conversation would not have been welcomed.

They came back near the shop and Jacie was outside cheering on the runners. James felt his legs want to speed up when he saw her and had to dial back his excitement since his partner would have been the only victim in such a surge. James didn't want to show off. Jacie leaned over to two people, James assumed it was her parents, and pointed at him. He figured out what was going on and did the politest thing he could without abandoning the race, he waved. They waved back. Off to a solid start. Skip laughed and grumbled, "Oh you kids.". James swore he saw a smile.

Music filled the streets, as did the smells of a variety of food trucks, which admittedly made the race even more difficult. They clipped off mile after mile and while James had no idea what pace they were going, he felt confident that they were doing good. He felt good. But then he realized he felt good, and wondered if that meant he was doing good – or if it meant he was going too slow and should be hurting. He didn't know the complexity of the marathon pain-per-mile math, so he just kept running.

The last mile saw a significant hill that both men had to dig deep to power up. After the hill, the course finished up with about a minute's worth of straight, flat, road – people cheering crazily for everyone. The pair cruised down the last straight together, neither one of them with victory over the other on their mind, victory was in getting done, not beating someone you weren't ever competing against to begin with. The last part was known as "Wave Alley", everyone was waving at you, and it was expected that you waved back (those who were truly competing got a pass on understanding). They felt like Olympians. People were going crazy for their success, desiring their recognition, and they were then happy to oblige them. Skip was no rookie to Wave Alley, but James was – but the feeling was never lost on Skip. Sixty meters from the finish line, James saw Jacie on the opposite side of the road and swerved over to give her outstretched hand a high-five.

And then, out of the corner of his eye, opposite of Jacie, light erupted from the crowd.

Boom.

27

An earthshaking explosion and hot flash threw James onto his back. His ears were ringing, and it was all he could hear. There was smoke in his immediate view, but he could see people running in every direction, he could see them screaming. He was in a haze, and it took him rather significant time to send messages from brain to body part to execute any action. Hoping to process where the explosion came from, he followed the trail of smoke to the side of the street he had just moved from. His head turned back toward where Jacie had been, she was jumping over the barrier to get to James when he yelled for her to stay back. He wasn't sure if anything came out of his mouth, but his arms flailed toward her as if saying, "Get out of here! Get to the shop!" who knew if there were other explosions to go off soon. He didn't know what had blown up, it could have been anything. Whatever had been there, malignant or benign, the damage had been done.

Bodies strewn out on the ground like an urban warzone, a description of what may have been – it was tough to say at that point. Skip writhed on the ground, rolling around on the cold cement. James willed himself off the ground and hobbled over to his friend and kneeled near him, trying to assess the damage he had sustained and how he could help with the little knowledge he had of such things.

All The Things That Could Be

He tried to get Skip's attention by calling his name in quick succession and guiding him, "Look at me. Where does it hurt?" James scanned the body and couldn't assess anything that was an easy roadmap to his source of discomfort. There was no question that Skip was in more pain than he had ever been in before, but James, in his frenzy, couldn't exactly tell where from. As he floundered there, he heard behind him another cry. By this time, people had rushed on to the course to assist the victims in all their various conditions. Many of them were fans and some of them were competitors. Sirens screamed in the distance; a cacophony of help raced on their way.

The man behind him wailed like a ghost, a noise that begged for help or death, whatever could come sooner. His injury was apparent as he saw the man in one spot and his lower arm in another location. A trail of red painted the street from one point to another. Having no medical know-how, there was only one thing he hoped would be a sufficient answer at the moment, James ripped off his shirt and started to make a tourniquet above the man's wound. He believed it would keep him from losing too much blood, but he wouldn't have bet the house that this was the reason to make one. He tied it as quickly and as tight as he could before scouring the area for something to cover the man up. He looked toward the smoke and saw abandoned pieces of blankets, coolers, and chairs – some were intact, but they weren't in great condition. He grabbed a blanket and put it over the victim.

All The Things That Could Be

The sirens rolled in with such fury James feared casualties from the help itself. EMTs, firefights, and police bailed out of their cars and others came full sprint from around the block – they all had one goal: find someone who needed help. James ran toward the oncoming wave and tried to signal where the man he was helping was located, furiously waving his hands and pointing in the direction. He also motioned to Skip who had found his way to one knee, but when James turned back around, Skip was back on the ground.

A woman in red ran toward James and slowed up as she approached – the look on her face turned to horror when she saw him. James noticed her olive skin and the tight bun that rested upon her head, and then his eyes closed, and he remembered no more.

***

He heard himself before he saw anything. Wherever he was, he knew he was not going to be leaving, not any time soon at least. James felt no less than four pieces of equipment connected to him. He was completely pain-free, which told him that he was either fine or in terrible shape.

He put all the puzzle pieces together and when he opened his eyes to white, fluorescent lights and boring rectangular tiles on the ceiling, with balloons in his periphery, he knew exactly where he was. A soft beep broke the silence intermittently, he guessed that the longer between beeps, the better. He groaned again when he moved his tongue, he realized that something was lodged down his throat.

He moved his eyes from side to side and tried to catch the attention of someone, anyone – just to let them know he was awake and alive. He had no idea of his condition or what anyone expected of him. He recalled seeing the look on the woman's face in front of him, and that was the last thing he remembered. He tried to think hard and fill in any gaps between then and now, but those moments in time in his brain were tabula rasa. As he remembered what happened, he tried to evidence gather by listening to the sounds around him. It was too calm to assume that the city was dealing with a full-on terrorist attack or anything of that magnitude.

A nurse hustled by his room and James raised a couple of fingers off the bed in hopes of catching her attention. She was purpose-driven and would not have noticed a skeleton tap dancing in the room. After passing by, James noticed he caught the attention of an administrative worker at the desk. Her eyes widened and she acted with haste to convey the movement to the doctors. James saw her get on a phone and bark her directions into it. Before long, a couple of nurses and a doctor were surrounding him.

All The Things That Could Be

Three? He felt like the higher the number, the worse the news was for him. He would have been happiest with one, but at least it wasn't the entire floor.

"Rise and shine, there." The doctor glanced over a chart at the end of the bed and the nurse checked the machines around James, making marks along the way. Unsure of his ability to talk, James made the same motion he made to attract the busy nurse, but in this case, it meant "hello." rather than "hello?".

The doctor told him they would be removing the tube that day, but he had been in there for a couple of days, placed into a medically induced coma because of the trauma inflicted by the attack. The word "attack" brought James relief and fear. Relief because he knew what happened. There were a lot of questions that James couldn't ask at the moment, but he knew his answers would be known in due time. The doctor went on about his condition, he was banged up pretty good, but nothing that would shelve him for too long. Staying in the hospital for a few more days would be to the benefit of everyone involved.

"You've had quite a few visitors so far; we told them your condition and they said they would come back. We gave a rough timetable of when we thought you would be in better shape. You have some fans out there, but admittedly, those people don't know a whole lot about you. A girl brought your cell phone into the hospital, and it was the biggest hope we had of finding any family to contact. We were perplexed about the lack of information and the girl told us a little bit of your story – it's a peculiar one." James felt like he was being lectured but wasn't sure if he was being scolded or not. It was not pragmatic to argue any points or contest anything he said since it would have taken him hours to respond. He then focused on the first part – quite a few visitors. "Nice!" He thought. Made the situation a little better.

He stewed in his thoughts after the doctor left. Eventually, they came in and removed the tube – no doubt one of the more peculiar feelings in his life. He managed to catch a look at himself from the reflection in a window and noticed the bandage over his head from the knock he took as he fell limp to the ground and smashed his head on the curb. It was the fall that caused doctors to induce him into a coma while his brain swelling eased.

He saw his phone near the bed and saw it was turned on but stuck at the passcode screen. "Guess the journey is over." He laughed to himself, if this were the end, it had been a good ride.

As he thought about the next step in his life, Jacie slowly approached his room – worried about what she might see, but elated with what she did see. She had to contain her energy because it was overflowing. His throat felt raw from the tube's presence, but he was happy to handle that pain as he made light conversation with her. She started by questioning how he was doing physically, then mentally and emotionally.

All The Things That Could Be

There was no way for him to gauge his emotional and mental state since he had so little information about what happened. This was a hint for her to clue him on what had indeed happened. The details were murky, she said. There was a belief that the local skinheads used the race to target Skip as a message about "their work in the community", James was able to break the code. The way she talked nonchalantly about Skip in the comment gave him confidence that Skip was doing fine. He asked anyway.

"What happened to Skip? The last thing I remember he was in the middle of the street writhing in pain." He presented the question in a calm manner that mirrored the demeanor of Jacie in her previous comment.

"Skip is fine. Apparently, it takes more than a pipe bomb to kill him – his words. He also made sure to say that the race took more out of him than the explosion did. But he was really worried about you. He has been in here more than anyone." This came as a shock to James, especially since if he had to bet, he would have thought it was Jacie who visited him more than anyone. He always recognized that may have been more of a wish, though.

"What? Truly?" Just to get some confirmation on the matter, James' raspy voice probed back.

"Well, second most." A smile appeared across her face, but it was a shy one that she didn't necessarily mean to show. James went to put his hands behind his head before realizing he was still connected to way too many machines.

Jacie then became a bit ashamed as her eyes locked onto the phone. "I am sorry that I went through your stuff to get your phone here. I knew you didn't want it on, but I felt like it may provide a little more information than I could give." He appreciated her apology, not because it was at all necessary, but because it was cute that she was so concerned.

"I appreciate you thinking of me in that way." Talking was getting easier, but it still felt like a chore. "Oh yeah, I am sorry that I missed meeting your parents." Jacie snorted and quickly covered her with her hand. James winked at her. "They will forgive you, in time. They are still here." She laughed.

"If you do stick around, I am sure that there is work you could find in the area." Jacie jumped back into the imminent future with her problem-solving ability. This felt wildly close to an invitation. James' poker face was strong — when he talked about going back home, it was merely to get her to show her hand, and she had. While they had only known each other for a brief time, he had no meaningful ties to anywhere else. Wilmington, Delaware was as viable of a landing spot as was anywhere. He still had enough money to stay afloat for a couple of months, if he couldn't find work. He wondered about the hospital bill. If you get attacked in a terrorist plot, do you still have to foot the bill?

"I would absolutely love to stick around. I still need to finish that marathon." Jacie moved closer and lightly grabbed his hand.

He finally came to the worst part of the conversation, a fact that he needed to know. "Did anyone die?" He asked the question in a way that was longer than it would have been in any normal circumstance. He hoped to be able to assess her face to brace for the worst if he noticed it when he asked it.

"No. There were injuries, a lot of them, but miraculously no one died. Oh. OH!" She started to vibrate. "I heard one of the medics talking about someone who made a tourniquet and saved a guy's life. Saved a life! Her words! And they pulled out the shirt and guess whose shirt it was? It was yours!" She pointed at him with both index fingers.

"Awesome." He did the lightest fist pump he could.

"How long until you are discharged?" The conversation steered back toward the immediate.

"He said to stay a few more nights. Just to make sure everything checks out." He recalled the conversation with the doctor. He was officially tired at this point. To speak was to labor.

"I am going to let some people know that you're doing well."

James stayed a total of one more week in the hospital as they made sure he was healthy enough to leave, given the injuries he sustained. Many visitors from the running group had come to see him. Skip visited often and the two decided they had unfinished business to attend to by finishing that marathon next year. Again, it felt like an invitation to stay.

Jacie stayed late the last couple of nights in the hospital with him. Before he was released, he decided to flip through the channels as the TV glowed in the room. He turned to the local news and watched to get some knowledge on the place he may soon call his own. A handsome anchor with slick black hair organized his papers as he brought up the final news story of the hour: two men, both affiliated with the local Aryan Nation, were found dead in the woods thirty miles outside of Wilmington. Anyone who had any information was encouraged to speak with the police.

Fat chance.

James turned off the television and fell into a deep slumber.

28

The sun pierced the curtains of the hospital room and James tried to block the light with this hand, but the attempt was pointless. He had finally gotten the okay to go home, the doctor going over all his injuries and what to look for, and "in case this happens, make sure you come back in." He thanked the doctor for his time and care and then began packing up his goods. He noticed his phone still on the table, a device that was so out of sight and mind that he didn't even think about it, much less think about using it.

For the entirety of the journey, he had promised not to use it. It was another old-world chain that he had hoped to cast off, and he did. But he was also curious if anyone had missed him and decided to show that in the way of a message or a voicemail. He didn't have a lot of friends back home, no one that he went out of his way to hold on to, so his expectations were low. But after he typed in the password to his phone and it finished booting up, a constant chime and vibration gave him a feeling that he didn't anticipate.

Messages flowed from people he once was close with, and people hardly talked with. He read through the messages, and it was made clear that the journey he had taken off on may have been misinterpreted as a result of self-loathing. While people may have been reaching out to him for the wrong reason, it was still a reason. It was an indicator that people did value him more than he anticipated. And

All The Things That Could Be

even if people were reaching out strictly because they feared for his life, it didn't matter to him. He was still happy to see how many people cared enough to check-in.

There would be a time and place to reply to these notes and a time and a place to set the record straight, but it wasn't right now. He would slowly reacclimate himself with a device, but he wasn't feeling the need or desire for current full immersion. He wanted to use it as a nice, useful commodity, not as a vital component of his life.

He gathered his belongings and left the hospital. He was greeted by a couple of members from the running club, namely Skip and Jacie. They went out to lunch and enjoyed some time with friends. There was an inquiry into what the next leg of James' journey would be. "What happens next? Where are you going to now, traveling man?" Skip asked between bites of food. It was a question that he had considered during his time in the hospital. He knew that any plans he made could be temporary for as long as he needed them to be, or until he focused on something permanent in an area. Skip didn't know much; Jacie knew a little bit more.

James didn't mean to come off as withholding or mysterious when he gave such a pause for his answer, but he also didn't want to seem too irrational or hasty when delivering such a potentially life-altering event. He also understood the irony in his hesitancy.

"Ya know, I think I am going to hang around here for a little while." His words reeked of ambiguity, but his voice hinted at more permanence. He went on, "I can find a place in the city and look for work. I could look for a teaching job or something similar. I don't know. I am sure there is something out there."

"There is a position open at the store if you want it," Jacie informed him excitedly.

"You're gonna let your girlfriend be your boss? Oh boy. Careful." Skip took a final drink and put the mug down. When he did, he saw how red both of their faces were. "Oh, come off it, if you aren't now, you're just a couple of days away from being." He ribbed.

"Thank you for that option. Something to consider." He didn't know enough about running and all its culture and intricacies to be effective there, that's not to say he couldn't learn.

His teaching certificate would move over, he did find that out. He felt calmer about the prospect of being back in the classroom, despite all the emotional luggage that sometimes came along with it.

There was certainly a renewed sense of self about him as he sat in that restaurant in Wilmington, Delaware, something that was not present at the beginning of his trip. A journey that started with his certainty that he lacked purpose and that it could be found somewhere else. He traveled that journey without a specific goal of what purpose would look like, but as he sat there among friends, he felt like he had found it. Not because of a potential budding relationship, which was a bonus, if it happened.

James reflected on his journey as he tried to find the moment when the switch happened, and he could not pinpoint the spot. It felt more like an amalgamation of all his journey's relationships which helped him better see himself as valued and purposeful.

29

"They weren't kidding about the darkness here." Jamaal took a bite off his plate, and like passing a basketball, gave the responsibility to someone else to figure out what to do next. It was not an astute observation, quite lazy, but it might work as a medium to jump-start the conversation.

Jamaal had been in Greenland for about four or five months by his immediate math. The fact that the sun never, or rarely, came up was otherworldly, he sometimes pretended he was living in another galaxy where this was normal. There were specific precautions they needed to take to ensure their body got the correct care, vitamin D supplementation and light therapy were the two big ones that the company got on them about.

Despite the low-hanging fruit conversation starter, his colleagues nodded quietly. They were taking a break as they tried to discover a substance or a thing, that would cause oil to break apart and dissolve in water, in the case of another oil spill, somewhere. There would be one, and then there would be another – every day they worked, they felt confident they were closer to the answer. Or at least an answer.

After the meal they departed back to their stations where they could collaborate on studying microorganisms and periodically adding them to oil-rich water and seeing what happened. There was a lot of failure in the work, and

All The Things That Could Be

Jamaal had to take it with a grain of salt because it only took one success to make all the failures worth it. He never got too excited, even when he thought he might have a hit on his hands. Getting excited just to be let down was a rookie mistake, and he learned quickly that it was the worst mistake you could make.

His coworkers felt like they were battling the darkness, rather than coexisting with it, rather than accepting it. While he had no issues with the darkness, he liked it, it certainly could turn the mood of others. This was something not anticipated when he came up. The longer they were up there, the more irritated he would see people become with the number of failures that kept stacking up and the endless literature they would read trying to solve the puzzle that so eluded them.

Jamaal noticed an uncharacteristic huddling around one of the stations near the end of the shift and slowly made his way over to investigate. As he drew near, he could make out a newspaper still on the front page. He got on his tiptoes and crooned his neck to see what the commotion was over. Finally, he interjected.

"What are y'all fawning over this time?" They all came from the States and the newspapers from home were delivered every so often, this one was about a month old. Their Internet was spotty at best, so the best they could do was what they got on an inconsistent basis. Typically, they would pass it around from person to person. There were

All The Things That Could Be

rules though, rules that were built on the go. The darkness did odd things to people, so when one of his new friends got the newspaper with the crossword already filled out, the lab nearly became a very expensive fight club.

On the front of the newspaper was a man tying a tourniquet for an armless man. Chaos and smoke around him. Jamaal knew his face but, at the moment, had a tough time placing him. He went through a mental Rolodex but very quickly found the file.

"Jimmy?" He squinted at the paper, the quality of the photo and quantity of blood could give some plausible deniability, but he was sure it was his old boss. He muscled his way into the crowd, breaking the agreed-upon procedures. Some people threw up their hands at Jamaal, but he didn't notice. He became enraptured in the photo and what was happening in it.

"Hey, come on now, what are you doing? Knock it off, Jamaal." The words came from one of them but were thought by all of them. They felt that he must have been pulling a joke on them, just not a very funny one.

"No, no, no…" Jamaal trailed off and used his hand to shush the rest of the dissenters. He picked up the newspaper and read quickly the text about the attack. Everyone sat in stunned silence as they let this new artist work in his medium. When he was done, he slowly lowered the newspaper and softly spoke, "This is my old boss. This is Jimmy. I told y'all about him during that meet and greet

All The Things That Could Be

week we had at the beginning. This is him." He kept tapping the photo.

Jamaal had mentioned this to the entire team about this boss who gave him a heads up that he was getting the axe at work and to polish up his resume. Refusing to let one of his own be fed to the proverbial wolves, he went out of his way to ensure his people were aware that ownership was looking to save a buck. He told them that the conversation was the launching point for getting him to where he was at that moment. The dialogue between employee and boss allowed him to plan ahead and with that extra time, he decided to look at jobs far and away, explaining his presence in Greenland.

Their eyes began to illuminate as one scrambled for the paper to get a look at the man, to find evidence in a caption, claiming that this man was the Jimmy of the tales. Meanwhile, Jamaal tried to envision the adventure that brought James to Delaware, to run a marathon, to have to tourniquet someone's arm, or what was left of it.

There were two conversations in the last year that he would always remember: the first was with James. The moment allowed him to pursue something else, out of necessity and moved him from the tracks of the do-nothing railroad. Especially, given his circumstances about what was found in his neck. The conversation was a small blip on someone else's radar, but a life-changing moment on his own. The second would be from the doctor a week or so later, the tumor was benign, but they should remove it anyway.

While the rest of the team pored over the newspaper, someone who had not joined the reading party erupted at their station.

"I think you guys are going to want to see this!" The newspaper was forgotten as they ran collectively to the excitement.

30

Dom stepped up to a rambler in the morning, cold from the previous night's unforgiving evening – Montana weather cared little for your housing situation. He rang the doorbell and heard the shuffling of feet and voices inside. He was familiar with the voices of the people inside, but he was very unfamiliar with the welcoming that would come from the other side of the doorway. He heard the door unlock and then it opened to a man who was a more put-together version of Dom. Despite being around the same age, he looked significantly younger.

"Hey, Paul." Dom greeted him, he hadn't seen Paul in roughly a year. He hadn't seen Paul's family in the same amount of time, his family, by extension. He only had seen through the screen of social media.

"Dom. This is a surprise. What do you need?" It was a coldly asked question and not one that upset or shocked Dom. Paul and anyone else in Dom's life had come to regard him as untrustworthy. Working back into a healthy trusted state was Dom's job to make happen, not something he should expect from anyone he had done wrong just because he was temporarily feeling better.

"I want to get clean." It was something that Dom had never said before, not to someone else and not to himself. When he heard it, his brother was silent. He looked Dom up and down and saw a cold and broken man. "When was the last time you used?" He asked Dom with a bout of sincerity in his voice.

"A few weeks ago. I have been off it since, not because I wanted to but because I didn't have any. I can tell you all about it if you want to hear." Dom looked over Paul's shoulder at a kitchen table. He wanted to come in and see his sister-in-law and their kids, but he also knew that inviting himself into their house after everything he did and everything he was, was a bold move, an inappropriate move.

Paul recognized the look but wasn't ready to take the dive – it still hurt Dom a bit, but he remembered it was his actions that got him to that point. It was also his actions and decisions that brought him to the door of his brother to beg for mercy. He put up a finger to Dom and shut the door, before emerging with a heavy jacket and his car keys. He also had a second jacket, which he thrust into Dom's chest. "Get in." Dom complied.

They went to a local coffee shop, a rustic, little building called "The Roaster" that harbored a couple of early morning customers with their laptops opened, headphones in, and hot drinks radiating next to them. Dom thought how nice it would be to be at that point of his life, where it was just school, maybe work, and coffee in front of him. Then he thought, maybe it could be one day.

The music was softly playing over the speakers and the warm lighting made the area a cozy den of coffee smells. Dom compared this to waking up in some houses that had no electricity for months, coming down from a high, and smelling vomit, among other things, all around him. He shook the thought out of his head, "I am not there anymore."

Paul motioned for him to sit down while he headed to the counter. The conversation and body language between Paul and the barista made it clear that he was a frequent customer here, and probably well-liked. He knew little about his brother's doings outside of the snapshots he saw online. Dom's eyes played about the room as he took in the place he wanted to be, in the state he wanted to be in. Before long, Paul came back with two drinks in his hand. He slid one across the table to Dom and said, "Peppermint."

The two chatted back and forth, and as they did Dom noticed that his honesty had a direct relationship as to how Paul received anything he said. He wasn't someone who felt too prideful, high, or sober, so he tried to be as honest as possible. Coming clean about his years of drug abuse and what he had to do to fund that life was tough to choke out. The visceral reactions, albeit subtle, that Paul gave to some of the things he said made Dom feel shame. Maybe he should have warned him first that there would be some ugly parts to the story. Better late than never, he reasoned.

"Paul, I am sorry, man. There are some ugly parts of my life. Things you're not going to want to hear, and things I'm not going to want to share." His brother respected the honesty and wondered if this truly was what the prayers of a broken man sounded like. Or he couldn't help but wonder, was this what the trap of a professional junkie looked like. Was he so desperate for money that he would concoct such an epic to be trusted again? The final blow?

His brothers always had a soft spot for him and always gave him the benefit of the doubt, even when they knew to do so was folly. Each time, however, they became a little more hardened. The conversation continued and Dom confessed some of his ugliest sins.

"Did you ever hurt anyone for money or drugs?" Paul demanded the answer point blank.

"No. Not physically, at least. I am sure my stealing and getting others addicted with me, so as not to feel so alone, hurt quite a few. But I have never physically harmed anyone for it." Dom confessed. Paul could see the hurt in his eyes and accepted the confession as fact.

Curiosity got the best of Paul, and well before he had planned to ask, a question came out that would steer the conversation and decision-making process for them both. "Why now? Why are you so intent on getting clean now?" Another question that immediately popped into his head immediately after asking was "Why would you want to start in the first place?" but that ship had sailed long ago.

The tale that Dom told about his life nearly being taken in a convenience store sounded like an episode of a television show, not a real-life event. He told it the best he could, and he told it true. He explained the car ride, the conversation, the event, and the conclusion. This man who he had met who saved his life using a can of cream of chicken, who could have just left him there and saved himself. Something changed in him, beyond the nearly meeting-your-maker-life-flashed-before-your-eyes event. He was shown selflessness, which directly conflicted with his own life, complete selfishness. A shared experience, a shared near-death experience, no less, was a changing one.

"I have never been a person who has been into signs or anything, but this backpack has been with me since school. It has hauled homework, stolen property, drugs, clothes, almost anything you can think of. I have had it for about 20 years now, and when I was trying to keep myself from being heard, it broke and fell on the ground. It betrayed me when I needed it most. It's almost like it was telling me 'You have misused me for the last time, it is time for you to make a change' and just like that, here I am." Dom felt as if he were rambling incoherently, but Paul was sticking to every word. He was truly impressed by the insightfulness his brother was delivering on. He had never seen this side of Dom, sober or not.

Paul felt guilt and remorse, as if, somehow, this brother's addiction and the years of his life that were lost and could never be returned, were his fault. He was laying out such ornate and detailed thoughts that it seemed like he was talking to a stranger. If this part of Dom was there the entire time, he had never taken time to notice it. He had stonewalled him enough that he never would have given him the chance to impress him. All of this, while understanding that he didn't want to be a sucker for a ploy.

The stories he told and the emotions he felt while delivering such sermons were exhausting. He had not required such mental fortitude for years, doing so now was physically taking its toll on the man. He put his head in his hands, and while Paul mistook it as being done out of sadness and grief, Dom was just so tired he needed some reprieve.

"Alright, man, how can I help you get clean? What do you need from me?" Paul felt that he already knew the answer to the question, it would be some combination of "money or a room". He was half right when the answer came across from Dom. "I need to get checked into some in-patient rehab. I have been around the game long enough to know the best ways of getting off the junk – that's the one. There is structure, support, accountability, camaraderie, and even captivity. I can't just leave if I want to. I need that." Paul would have given him all the money he had after hearing that answer, luckily, he had more than enough to cover a stint for his brother.

"Do you know where the nearest facili…" Paul couldn't even get the entire question out of his mouth before the answer arrived.

"The best is in Bozeman, it's not the nearest but it's the best." Paul's stare pierced through him. He felt like he was getting his brother back, but a better version of that brother. Or, perhaps it was the version that was always there, just caked behind the drugs and the walls that had been constructed so people wouldn't be hurt.

"When do you want to go?" Paul wanted another answer to fill him with pride and certainty that his brother was serious about this endeavor.

"I wish I were there right now. I just need to call and check availability." James began to dial. There was space available – a few spots. So, if they drove out there today or tomorrow, he would be in a good spot to pick one up. "I know I have asked a lot of you, but can I ask you one more thing? Drive me out there and check me in." Paul stood up, which caused Dom to stand up. They hugged for the first time since either of them could remember.

"Will you tell Henry you saw me? Will you tell him when I get back that I did it?" Dom asked Paul in the embrace. The response was muted, but he heard more in his brother's wet nodding than anything he could have said. "Yeah buddy, I will."

The two drove back to the house and Dom waited in the car while Paul went inside to let the family know of the change of plans in his day. Paul's wife was incredibly supportive of the trip, as she had once suffered from addiction abuse. No one knew the journey better than her. The kids filtered into the kitchen to get the story and then asked where Uncle Dom was, assuming he was still at the coffee shop or a store in town. "He is in the car, waiting for me. I just need to grab him some clothes for the trip." He turned to head to the room.

"Can we go see him?" Paul stopped dead in his tracks and defaulted to his wife. He knew the answer he wanted to give, but he didn't want to give an answer based on feeling if it wasn't the right one. She smiled and nodded.

Dom's three nieces and nephews barreled out the front door and clamored for him to get out. Despite all the horror that Dom had inflicted on those around him, he always tried his best to be portrayed as sober and with it to his nieces and nephews. They knew he struggled with stuff, but they knew of it as stuff, nothing particular. Dom ejected himself out of the front seat and opened his arms to the oncoming horde. They wrapped their small bodies around him and asked how long he was staying.

"Guys, Uncle Dom is a bit sick right now. I am going to go to a hospital to get better." This started a tirade of them trying to guess what was broken, what disease he had, or what surgery was necessary. "I will tell you all about it when I come back, nice and healthy." At that moment, Paul came out of the house with a bag packed with his own belongings for Dom. They all said their goodbyes and Dom and Paul got into the car and pushed east.

***

All The Things That Could Be

Dom's time at Ranch Recovery was enlightening but didn't come without challenges. He still yearned for the junk from time to time. Sometimes the yearning pushed over into feeling obsessed. However, he now possessed methods to handle the feeling of needing it. He knew how to talk to someone; he knew how to push back those urges from the counseling he had received and the learning he had accepted. He felt it would never get easier, which made it tough, but he felt he could always overcome it if he did what he had learned. He felt as if his accountability net could be big enough to support him. He would not go back into the world as someone who had no believers.

The day he received his ninety days sober token (he started his timer the day he showed up at Ranch Recovery instead of racking his heroin brain for the exact date of his last high) he stopped in the common room on the way back to his room. He sat on the sofa with some of the other patients as they surfed through the channels, looking for something interesting to end their night. Eventually, the remote wielder stopped on the news to the displeasure of many. Groans filled the room and others decided that turning in early beat watching the news.

Two anchors sat next to one another, and while a handsome man looked over at the handsome woman, a serious expression broke over her powdered and done-up face. The camera switched to show only her, the over-the-shoulder graphic, and the headline "Marathon Terror Still Unknown". The patients sat in silence as they focused on the story – none of them seemed to be privy to this incident. Someone came into the room loud and boisterous before being "shhh!-ed" by the rest of the ground.

"There is still little information about the cause of the bomb which went off at the Wilmington Marathon. Local police have said that the event is still under investigation and that when they find out more, they will let it be known. But locals aren't as sure that there is much mystery." The camera switched to a woman who said, "It's that Aryan Nation group, those skinheads that came from Penn! They are rallying here. Everyone in the town knows it's them. Police know it's them, they just haven't had one of those cowards admit it yet." The camera cut back to the anchor. "This bomb exploded near the finish line on Sunday, a photographer working for the Associated Press managed to capture this scene." On the screen, a picture flashed on the screen which resembled a warzone captured the attention of them all.

Dom jumped out of his seat and ran to the screen. He obscured the vision of most of the viewers and they started to jeer him. They were confused about his interest in it, as he was unresponsive to the jeering he was receiving. He was acting out of character. "Hey! Dom…DOM!" Shouted someone as the photo hung on the screen.

"Pause it!" Dom barked back and then the wielder used his power to seemingly freeze time.

"What is it, man?"

"What do you see?"

"Bro, are you high *in* treatment?"

He was very calculated and sure about what he saw in the picture: a shirtless man who was tying a tourniquet onto the stump of an arm that belonged to a screaming man. The shirtless man was looking directly at the camera but not in it, as if he had no idea it was there. He knew absolutely that he had seen that man. He knew that it was James.

"I know this guy!" His face shot back at the rest of the patients, and he knew he had to act quickly. "No seriously. This is the guy from the gas station robbery. This is James! No joke. I am sure." Disbelief flooded the faces of those in the room. Sometimes in these places, people try to make themselves out to be more than they are. Some people waved him off and rolled their eyes.

"What? You mean the dude from here in Montana? He was in this marathon out in Delaware? Ain't no way, man." One of his fellow addicts shot back, he had remembered well.

Dom tried to recount why this could have been James but a lot of them laughed it off and ended up standing up, stretching, and giving some rendition of "Well, that's enough of that for tonight! Time to hit the hay!" Dom didn't need them to believe him, that wasn't important to him. One woman who had been in the program for less than a month hung around. "I believe you." she softly admitted.

James sat down next to her and just stared at the frozen screen taking in what he was seeing. He laughed and pointed back to the television. "That is the dude who got me in here. When I knew him, he wasn't covered in blood and was wearing a shirt." She laughed.

He hit play on the remote and finished the story. He listened for James' name but it was never revealed – not that he needed it for any sort of validation. "Multiple casualties but no deaths, miraculously, were reported." The anchor's somber tone was going to transition soon because sports was up next.

"No deaths? That dude's arm was blown off. James saved that guy, too. My god. He has saved two lives." He was quite excited about this and trying to pass off his excitement to the new tenet, who said nothing but, "he sounds like a pretty good guy."

Retiring to his room, Dom lay in his bunk and wondered what would have happened if James just kept on driving, if they hadn't stopped for gas, or if his backpack hadn't broken in the one moment that he needed it not to break.

All The Things That Could Be

***

'Coffee up – Henry!" Dom's voice carried throughout the shop. He at once regretted calling "Henry", when he could have said something much more clever to razz his brother. Henry approached the counter and grabbed the drink off the counter. "Dom, see you tonight at Paul's?" Dom had a headset on and put his hand over the mic and mouthed "Yeah."

"I'm sorry, can you repeat that order?"

Dom managed to stay clean after Ranch Recovery and moved into an apartment near Paul to spend more time with his family and make up for lost time. He managed to snag a job as a barista and put his obsessive personality into making exquisite coffee. He started to read about coffee, not just basic know-how stuff that he needed to be successful there but also the history of it, different blends, preparation types, and much more. He became an aficionado of it and became a bit of the go-to guy about coffee in Drummond.

Every day was a battle, but the was easier now than it had ever been. He had a support net and a purpose that didn't begin and end at jamming a needle into his veins and hoping for the best. He worked hard to stay clean and reaped the benefits of it – including but not limited to constant communication with his family that was not made with walls constructed and bad intentions assumed.

All The Things That Could Be

All The Things That Could Be

31

As those executives were walked out of the building in handcuffs, Molly felt a mix of elation and fear. Watching Heath getting his just desserts was enough to satiate her sweet tooth for years to come. She smirked at him and got as close as she could to make sure he saw it, then she winked to drive it home. His eyes darted from her mockery right back to the ground.

What Molly didn't know was she had discovered that Potrix and Ajax had been involved in highly illegal forms of labor control, salary fixing, corruption, and a bunch of other fancy words that were on the news. In short, the two worked to conspire to ensure that any union efforts were delegitimized and make the members lose faith in them. Break the union, and you can reject any person who comes to you groveling for a salary increase, instill disbelief, and reap the profits. How they were conspiring with one another was of great interest to the NLBR, and a more complete investigation put both companies on their heels, caused a dissolution of both of their Boards, and saw the top executives in jail, or some of them fled to non-extradition countries. It was massive.

All the media and the attention were stressful for Molly, it was more than she wanted to take on. She was lauded as a labor hero, after she then successfully negotiated with an arbiter, who, it was said, hated Potrix and Ajax as much as anyone else and gave them hell in the meetings. She never experienced that, but she had secured a package deal more than she could have hoped for. Did the arbiter help her out in this? Maybe. Was she going to ask questions? Absolutely not.

The win didn't belong to her, she would start off at the announcement of the new contract, but to union workers everywhere. She mentioned a friend who helped work through some boring and gritty work to help expose the corruption and "blow the top off of the entire thing." James Dalley would always be a friend to labor and workers everywhere. If Joe Hill were still around, surely, he would have written a song about him.

She ended up stepping down from her position and moved back to Jacksonville and worked at a local market, far away from the massive corporations that stole the souls and wages from workers. On the side, she worked to train local union leaders and spread the good message of union labor. She worked tirelessly with the people to raise the standard of living for those who produced. "All we want is our share of the pie." was a saying she often went with when meeting with like-minded people.

Her work with local leaders and labor groups became famous throughout Florida, as she helped create problems for the right-to-work crowd. "They only win if you let them. If you stand in solidarity, you can get what you deserve. Sometimes if you want your piece of the pie, you need to take your piece of the pie." The more she traveled and the more she saw, the more it radicalized her. Molly visited areas untouched by wealth except for the fact that wealthy people had exploited the people of that community for profits. The more and more she saw this, the more she lamented the ideas of the system she was raised with. Changes needed to happen. She secretly confided to her diary that "workers would be in a better position if they were able to construct gallows on every factory floor and walk executives by them once a week."

Smart enough to know what would take and the messages that the common worker was willing to stomach was key to her position. She stuck to things that were not so radical but pushed the envelope in smaller settings. She saw herself as a farmer, throwing out seeds into smaller gardens to see if the soil was ready for them, rather than wasting her time trying to cultivate an entire field with something that may not take.

Her popularity continued to grow, and she knew she was hitting it big when anti-labor forces were attacking her in the press, on the radio, and on TV. When she left Potrix, it was in part because of her desire to avoid the limelight, but she found herself thrust right back into it. She didn't feel like she could avoid fate twice and didn't shy away from the opportunity this time.

Her regional influence morphed into a national one and she gathered a following of true believers. Before long, she was giving interviews and writing articles for any publication that would give her a chance. Molly traveled from city to city, state to state, hall to hall, to talk about organization. She always rattled off facts and figures that proved you were better off in unionized labor than the opposite. She even had to chance to go from house to house to meet with people who were recently unionized. The life was fulfilling.

On one chilly morning, Molly woke up to a message on her phone that she was being recognized by national leadership for her part in influencing union rates. Because of her participation and since she began her national work, union membership had jumped twenty percent in the public sector and forty percent in the private sector. Whether through causation or by coincidence, nationwide spending on non-vital goods was up, and there was an increase in home ownership (and a decrease in renting). Surveys showed that people were happier and fewer people were living paycheck to paycheck. When she called to get more information about this recognition, she was told that her work was making a difference on a national, but more importantly, on an individual level.

When receiving her award, the speaker referred to her as "The Daughter of Bill", which didn't bother her much, because even though they were referring to Bill Haywood, her father's name was Bill, so it worked on a couple of levels. She would never want to renounce her father, and now she didn't have to reject the *nom de guerre* in front of the crowd.

All The Things That Could Be

The speaker heaped praise on what she had done for the cause, but she knew she wasn't alone. There were plenty of people who helped her along the way, who helped her help others. She didn't pretend to be like those she fought against, pretending to be the only one who mattered in the outcome. She thought of James, and that was where the speech began. "My journey is our journey. There is no 'my' success in this movement, there is only 'our' success. This journey and success of labor started with a sandwich."

32

The unlikely prospect of settling down in Wilmington, Delaware after nearly getting blown to pieces in a marathon had been just that, unlikely. But it sure wasn't impossible. James sipped coffee on the back porch with his fiancé as she pored over sales from the store. Education became his chosen profession once more, as he sought out others to help, knowing that his actions could cause change in the lives of others, even if those changes were small. Sometimes you get lucky and can affect someone on a bigger level like the other week someone came into the store while James was hanging out and identified himself as the son of the man whose life he had saved by tying off the tourniquet. He expressed his appreciation to James, and he talked about the moment and James in reverence, "My dad loves to tell the story, funny enough. It is like his war story."

The man paused to see how James was reacting, he didn't want to open old wounds. He had calculated the amount of the story he would tell to fall short of that line. James looked uneasy not because of the event but because he had a tough time accepting praise for doing the right thing. The man had driven up from Kentucky to have the conversation. He admitted that he could have called but he felt, given what happened, a phone call would simply not have sufficed. "I needed to do this in person." He claimed.

All The Things That Could Be

"I do appreciate the gesture, that was very kind of you to go out of your way. But I am sure he would have done the same for me." James replied with a smile.

"I know that you are being humble about this, but you don't know how much good you have done. My dad has six grandchildren, and he is deeply involved in all of their lives. Without him, there would be a lot of missed opportunities and sad faces. So, once again. Thank you." The man was no longer just being pleasant and accepting the modesty that was being put out there by James. It was important to him that he understood the gravity of his actions. There would be understanding.

Understanding the shift in his demeanor, James responded in kind, "Tell your dad he is welcome; it was my pleasure to help. Make sure when he tells the story, he lets people know that I was really ripped." They both laughed. James felt it was weird and inappropriate to ask, "Why didn't your dad come with?" as it may seem like James thought he should have been there to thank him. Perhaps, this was just the son's thing he felt he needed to do.

They talked a little more as customers filtered in and out of the store. A cash register beeped, a bell rang, conversations were had, and questions were answered. Eventually, the man left. He may have had other business in the area or may have just come up to say thank you, no one knew, and no one asked. The conversation sat with James, however. The gratitude he was shown was a marker of the importance of his actions.

The year rolled along and eventually, Jacie and James would tie the knot before leaving on a month-long honeymoon in Nigeria and Ghana. When they returned, recharged but also longing for more time with less labor, the mail had stacked up significantly. The "unsure what to do with this" pile was leaning from so many envelopes and magazines. They sorted through them all and James noticed two envelopes that were specifically attention-ed to him via The Running Place. Jacie gave him a funny look and realized that James was wearing the same look as she. He opened the letters, first was a blue envelope with tough to distinguish cursive adorning the card's front. Jacie tucked in next to him and her eyes followed along as he read aloud:

James –

I am not sure if this letter will ever find you, but I am going to write it anyway and send it to where I think it could find you. Almost a couple of years ago, you picked me up on the side of the road where I was desperately trying to go and buy drugs in Deer Lodge. My name is Dom Haywood. That night, we got into a crazy scenario with a man who ended up trying to execute me on the floor of a gas station, and you ultimately smashed his head in with a soup can. That sentence was as weird to write as that night was to live.

After our night, I decided to abandon my quest and look to receive help with my addiction, rather than continue it. The short of it is, that I am still clean today. I saw you on the news when I was in rehab (it actually made me look crazy, high, or both) and I told everyone that that was you — they were familiar with who you were because my road to recovery story started because of you.

I am not sure if I will ever be able to thank you properly for the grace and empathy you showed me that night, or for the accuracy of your arm and your willingness to help a person who most people looked at as a dreg of society. I am now clean, working, and enjoying time with my nieces, nephews, and family — something that I have not been able to do for years, because of the trail of disappointment that I would leave behind.

We were both on a journey of sorts that night, and I want you to know that your journey helped guide mine to a more successful detour. I feel eternally grateful for us crossing paths.

Dom Haywood

***

"That was nice." James smiled at the letter.

Jacie popped him with an open hand on the shoulder. "Nice? Nice? Boy, that was amazing. How do you read that and just say 'nice'? Read the other one." Jacie now understood the temperament of the man who drove up to say thank you on behalf of his father.

All The Things That Could Be

James cleared his throat and got ready for the next letter. Secretly, he loved getting this mail. The validation was so good to hear. He would never admit that the recognition brought him joy.

James —

I read about you in the newspaper a couple of days ago (who knows when this was written, the envelope had been stamped "Return to Sender" a couple of times, with a new address slapped over the previous one) *and it was incredible. It was incredible in part because of how you helped me so selflessly during the strike. Then, I read about this guy who saves another guy's life amid a volatile (to say the least) situation. I was impressed but I wasn't surprised.*

I wanted to write to express my gratitude for your work with the strike and the endless hours you put into a project that wasn't even yours. At first, everyone was perplexed by your willingness to take on something and be part of something like this that would have no immediate impact on you. I am not sure how much, if any, you have followed what happened afterward but it has set off a ripple effect that is changing the ways industries can operate with their employees and the unions they are a part of. The whole thing was rotten to the core, and because of your eye, because of that serendipitous moment, workers across America are making more money and living better lives.

Because of everything, I ended up moving into a position of union leadership where I am helping unions around the country expand.

All The Things That Could Be

We are doing great things in this regard and are bringing more prosperity to working-class people everywhere.

When you left and went on your way east, you may not have ever known the impact that you would end up having on our community, on myself, and on the nation — but I am here to tell you that your efforts have caused huge gains for people across the country.

I hope that you are doing well, and I hope that we meet again one day. I hope this message finds you within a proper time.

All the best,

Molly

***

James didn't need to look to know that Jacie was looking at him with her hands on her hips in her "I told you so" pose.

All The Things That Could Be

Epilogue

The world was changing. Perpetually. It was changing because of climate, poverty, war, disease, wealth, cures, togetherness, to name a couple of things. It was changing in a good way some days and in a worse way other days. Nations and armies made gains in areas that they had never owned before, which would enrich one group of people at the expense of another. Most of the time, these changes were zero-sum.

Sometimes the changes were local, personal, and equally world-changing – when the butterfly's motions reached another part of the world, thousands of miles from its origin point. James Dalley read the letters from Dom and Molly at least once a week – not to stroke his own ego, but to remind himself the importance of his actions: no matter how small they were.

In the classroom, he did his best to be cognizant of his words and actions, impressionable students were most likely to see the heaviest of waves from his potential words and actions. That went for the good things…and bad ones. Not a perfect man in any regard, but he managed quick reconciliation whenever he had potentially set off negative waves, which could have reached Tanzania within the hour, or even just Pennsylvania.

One day during a lesson gone awry, Mr. Dalley ended a lesson by preaching a bit of a life lesson, "the things you do, the way you treat others – they have far-reaching impacts that you could not fathom to see right now. Nineteen-year-old Gavrilo Princip could not have ever dreamed of the changes he would make and how his actions would reverberate throughout history. Hopefully, you aren't assassinating world leaders, but you have unabridged power to change history."

The bell rang, and the class left.

"Thanks, Mr. Dalley! Have a good day!" A couple of students said as they filed out into the Wild West that was a public school hallway.

"Yup yup, you, too! Do good out there." James waved back.

"Yessir!" They disappeared into the crowd, hopefully ready to be helpers. James could only hope.

As he went back to his desk, he glanced one time at his computer. A message had come through in the hour from an email he didn't recognize – an out-of-district sender. He bent down and looked at the subject before deciding whether it was worth sitting for. He saw the subject: "Jimmy". He opened the message and read it under his breath.

Jimmy –

Hope this message finds you well, boss. Just wanted to drop in and say hello after a bit. I've been really busy, I just got back from Greenland where we discovered some bacteria that breaks oil down in salt and fresh water, and the best part is that it's easy to duplicate the

All The Things That Could Be

bacteria. There is some really promising stuff that is going to be announced recently, and I wanted to let you know first. You helped kickstart my career in biotech when you told me that Pam was gonna get rid of me, I appreciate you buying that time for me, I needed it.

I remember that you used to talk about how the world was full of bad news. Everywhere you looked, bad news on his channel, bad news on the Internet, bad news here, there, and everywhere. Now, I am not saying you're right, but there is good news out there too. It may be tucked way back in the back pages, but you know that stuff doesn't sell!

Good things are happening everywhere, I know you know this because I saw what you did out there in Delaware (Also, Delaware? Come on, man). I bet that dude you saved was sure glad you were there, and it may not be in the news, but every time he wakes up and does whatever he does, it's gonna be good news.

Jamaal

He closed his laptop while smiling. He thought if he should tell Jacie about this or not. She would feel right and rub it in his face.

Good things were happening for so many people in his life, and he just felt lucky enough to know about it. The good news was out there, Jamaal was right, sometimes we just have to make sure we are creating it ourselves.

Milton Keynes UK
Ingram Content Group UK Ltd.
UKHW021100080824
446563UK00016B/798

9 798218 465513